The Slumber of Consciousness

Alex O. Harb

The Slumber of Consciousness

Book Cover by Alex O. Harb
First edition 2026

ISBN 979-8-9992133-5-8 (Ebook)
ISBN 979-8-9992133-6-5 (Paperback)

https://alexoharb.site

Table of Contents

PART 1: THE PATTERN

CHAPTER 1

Protests

Henrik stood at his office window with his back to the door when she knocked. One hand on the glass, eyes on something outside. A crayon drawing sat on the windowsill – a six-year-old's house with a yellow sun, its paper curling at the edges.

"Close the door, Maren."

She closed it.

"I got a call this morning from upstairs. They want you off the lobbying investigation." He sat down and adjusted his glasses. "The lawyers went through the sourcing again, and the insurance carrier flagged us for defamation exposure."

"The sourcing was solid, Henrik."

"I know it was." He picked up a manila folder and turned it over in his hands without opening it. "I did push back. The conversation I had was – look, I told them we had documentation for every claim. What I was told was, pull it or they escalate to the board." He pushed the folder across the desk to her. "Protest coverage. Crowd photos, demographic summaries, the purist series."

“I’m not firing you, Maren.” He sighed. “See if there’s something with these protests worth Monday’s front page.”

“I did fight for you on this,” he added in a quieter voice. “I want you to know that.” He adjusted his glasses again.

She took the folder and walked out without a word. Past Lars, past the designers, past the empty desks with their dark monitors. A floor-cleaning robot hummed along the baseboard near the archive room, its brush spinning against the carpet edge. She made it to her own desk and sat down too hard – the chair rolled back and knocked the partition wall.

Lars glanced up. She pulled the chair forward and set the folder down. Opened her laptop, looking past it. Her jaw ached. She’d been clenching it since Henrik’s office.

Her expensive monitor stood on the desk, never used and covered with dust. The Cavling award leaned against it, where she’d put it two years ago instead of finding a proper place on the wall. Both were equally prestigious and equally useless, just as her investigation had become. She scrolled through the open document, then closed it.

Around her, the newsroom went on. Two reporters near the window argued over a caption. A designer in huge headphones tilted her head at a layout, getting the contrast right. *Berlingske* still printed in black and white, the last paper in Copenhagen that did. Others had switched to color or decided to chase readers online. Neither saved them. The Ritzau wire screen by the foreign desk was scrolling – another orbital launch, the thirty-eighth this year. Someone had left a half-eaten *rugbrød* on the desk across from hers, the cheese sweating. Two floors down, in the old production wing, the Heidelberg press rumbled through its afternoon run. She could feel it in the floor, a low, steady pulse. Or it was a train passing underground.

Kasper had texted that morning while she was walking from Kongens Nytorv to the building, scarf pulled up against the wind. He never texted out of the blue. She'd meant to reply before the morning meeting. Then the lobbying data pulled her in, then Henrik called her in, and the day went somewhere else entirely.

She went to the bathroom. Locked the stall. Called Sofie Brandt.

It rang five times and went to voicemail. The beep came while she struggled for words.

"Sofie, it's me. They killed it." She hung up.

Called again. This time she didn't speak. Five seconds of dead air, the bathroom fan humming. Someone had stuck a Post-it to the stall door: *Please don't flush paper towels.* She hung up.

She imagined Sofie crying, *You said the paper would protect me. You said that, in my kitchen, with my daughter in the next room!*

She washed her hands. The tap ran cold.

The kitchen nook smelled of old milk and stale food. Maren pressed the coffee machine button and stood with her arms crossed while it poured.

Lars from the foreign desk came in. Tall, reddish stubble. He opened the fridge, stared at the contents, and closed it.

"Saw you in Henrik's office." He leaned against the counter. "The lobbying piece?"

"Mm."

He glanced at her hands on the mug. She loosened her grip.

"You look like you're about to do something stupid," he said.

"I'm fine, Lars."

"Right." He opened the fridge again, as if the contents might have changed. "Someone keeps leaving yogurt in here with no name on it. I've been eating it." He closed the fridge. "Listen. If you need to decompress later, I'm heading to Ørsted at six. Off the record."

"I have work to do."

He nodded. Tapped the counter, took the yogurt, and left.

The coffee was burnt and acidic. At least now she knew what had happened to her yogurts.

Maren went back to her desk and opened the folder.

The purist protests. Timelines, locations, crowd estimates – the folder had it all laid out. The movement had started small and metastasized across Europe over the past year. Dock workers, editors, teachers. All of them marching under the same banner now. Against AI taking their jobs.

She logged into the paper's archive. Half the paper's correspondents were covering a burning topic: a Brussels defence committee investigating a case where defence AI had caused a confrontation in the Baltics – two governments describing it in mutually incompatible ways, the third not describing it at all. Maybe the purists weren't entirely wrong.

She scrolled down to the protest coverage. Faces, signs, crowd density. She'd been at this for twenty minutes when she switched to the live Ritzau feed to check today's Christiansborg march. The photos were still coming in, untagged, unsorted. She flicked through them, looking for usable crowd shots.

Her hand stopped.

A man in a green jacket, third row, half-hidden behind a woman with a placard. Not chanting, not holding a sign. Hands in his pockets, chin up. She knew that posture.

Kasper. She hadn't seen her brother in almost three years – since their mother's funeral in Odense. He was broader than she remembered, the jacket tight where it used to hang loose. Twenty-four years old, standing in a purist crowd in Copenhagen on a Wednesday afternoon. And texting her on the day of the protest.

Her hand lingered on the mouse, then the image went to a personal folder.

She plunged into the work: dates, cities, estimated attendance. Cross-referenced against the wire feeds.

Prague first, because the photos were recent and well tagged. It was a Wednesday. Students outside the Ministry of Digital Affairs, maybe sixty of them with printed signs. She was scanning the shots for crowd estimates when the background caught her. The tram lines running past the Ministry were empty – no trams in any of the four photos, the stop displays dark, the platforms bare. Central Prague, midday Wednesday, and the entire tram network was gone from the frame.

She pulled the Czech wire for that week. The rail authority had shut down every electric train and tram in the country for nine hours. *Central dispatch software fault*, the press release said.

The protest permit listed the organizing group as a philosophy society. Nothing about rail infrastructure.

She let that sit for a moment. Then went back to the wire feeds and started checking other cities.

Frankfurt took ten minutes. She cross-referenced the protest date against the Reuters roundup and found the sidebar: a power surge had knocked 200,000 households in Hesse offline for six hours. The purist march had been on a Monday. The outage had been on a Monday.

Cairo took longer. Dock workers were blocking the entrance to a logistics hub, protesting automated cranes and loaders – about forty of them. Same day, six hundred kilometers south, the Benban solar complex tripped offline. Rolling blackouts across three governorates for fourteen hours. The official cause was buried in a report she had to pull from the Egyptian grid authority's site: sensor malfunction in the inverter array. Dock workers in a port city had nothing to do with solar panels in the desert. She checked the local social feeds from that week and found thousands of shares of similar posts. *While blue-collar workers protested against AI taking their jobs, the AI-managed grid went dark across three provinces. Where are we heading now?*

She opened a new spreadsheet. Protest date, city, subject, matching outage. Prague. Frankfurt. Cairo. She pulled more. Warsaw matched: teachers marching against AI grading, same day the diagnostic network at the city's largest hospital crashed. Sixteen hours on paper charts. And similar activity on social networks.

Lyon. Purist march, a hundred people. Same day: nothing. She checked Reuters, AFP, the local feed. Clean.

She held on that. Lyon broke the pattern.

She pulled more entries. Most matched. Some didn't. Fourteen cities. Eleven correlations within twenty-four hours. Three clean. And every failure filed as a malfunction. Equipment faults. Software errors. Firmware updates.

Things that happen. The kind of things that get you a paragraph on page nine and a shrug from the foreign desk. Except for the social activity that framed every single case as "Look where it gets us." Bots, for sure, but it landed well – numbers of sympathizers skyrocketed.

Her thoughts returned to Kasper. She opened the Frankfurt photos and started checking them one by one. He was in the third photo. Right edge of the frame, half-turned from the camera, pixelated. Green jacket. Hands in his pockets. Same posture. October 29th.

The purist protests were local chapters, neighborhood marches. Her brother had been in Copenhagen that afternoon and in Frankfurt sixteen days earlier, five hundred miles from home.

She went back to the other cities. Scrolled through Cairo, Prague, Warsaw. The photos were lower resolution, the crowds smaller. She couldn't spot him. But two cities were enough.

Maren leaned back in her chair, looking at the files and the spreadsheet. The last row was Copenhagen. Today. The Christiansborg march. The outage column was empty.

Her phone buzzed. It was a smart home controller reporting a power loss. She opened a news alert in a new tab. DR, the state broadcaster: *Widespread grid disturbance across eastern Denmark. Outages spreading in central Copenhagen, Frederiksberg, Amager. Multiple districts without power. Energinet is investigating.*

She read it twice. Looked at the spreadsheet, then switched to a social network. The posts were already there. *Thinking machines are ruining our lives. They control our cities, our energy grids, our weapons!*

Maren picked up her phone and called Kasper. It went to voicemail.

She grabbed her coat and walked out of the newsroom. It was not a time for footwork yet, but she desperately needed fresh air.

CHAPTER 2
Row One

Tomás walked the São Paulo streets with the envelope heavy in his jacket pocket.

Carolina wasn't wrong about him. She had told the mediator as much. About the traffic light on Rua Augusta that had cycled green-yellow-red-green-yellow-red in two seconds flat. He'd driven past it, then turned back and visited it every day for two weeks. Probably a wiring fault, a power surge, or a trick of the afternoon light. Yet he'd spent an extra forty minutes every day taking this route to see if it repeated. And countless nights scanning the internet for similar cases. All while his ex-wife was scrolling through medical databases for a different word. Carolina had used it during the custody mediation – *fixação* – and her lawyer had written it down.

Vila Madalena to Pinheiros, forty minutes on foot, twenty longer than the metro. But walking delayed arrival, and arrival meant the apartment, and the apartment meant sitting with nothing left to do. The jacket had been right for the mediator's office and was wrong for everything since. The November sun sat heavy on the back of his neck, unmoving, pressing down. His shirt was sticking to his shoulders by Rua Fradique Coutinho. The streets gave him somewhere to put his eyes: fruit vendors stacking mangoes into pyramids on wooden carts, yellow-green in the sun. An autonomous delivery pod hummed past on the sidewalk, swerving around a dog that slept on warm concrete, one ear twitching at flies.

His thoughts drifted to the envelope. The edge of it pressed through his jacket lining.

Two women argued about a parking space with a fury that looked like it had a decade of history behind it. The block ahead was all consulting firms and co-working spaces, glass fronts catching the light. A bus shelter ad showed a rocket silhouette and the words *Órbita Brasil – seu satélite, sua órbita*. A man in a dark suit stood outside one of them, checking his phone.

The envelope held the custody resolution. Final mediation agreement, stamp, sixty-three pages with his name and Carolina's on the same line. He hadn't opened it since the mediator's office. It burned in his pocket anyway.

Jorge's printing shop was on a side street off Rua Aspicuelta. The sign said *GRÁFICA CLARA* in a nice script. The L was already gone, the screw holes still there. The door was propped open with a box of paper stock that wasn't going anywhere. There used to be a bell connected to the door frame, now replaced by a presence sensor.

Jorge came from the back when he heard the sensor buzz. He had a cloth over one shoulder, his hands wiped but not clean, the stain worked into the creases of his knuckles from years of handling stock. He looked thinner than on the last visit. "Senhor Herrera." Warm, unsurprised.

He made coffee without asking – a moka pot on a single burner behind the counter, the ritual already underway before Tomás was inside. A calendar on the wall was two months behind. He poured into ceramic cups, small, brown-glazed, the ones you brought out for people. He set one in front of Tomás and left his own on the counter while he wiped the counter with a cloth that was already clean.

"How's Lúcia?"

"Good. Making friendship bracelets now."

"Ah." He smiled. "My niece went through that. Bracelets on every surface, all over the house. I still have one in the shop somewhere – the thread's gone brown." He spread his hands. "What do you do with them after?"

Tomás said he hadn't thought that far ahead. They were in Carolina's house anyway.

They talked. Jorge remembered his daughter's name and age without Tomás having to reintroduce her. Then he mentioned a nephew – his wife's brother's son, learning web design on YouTube, getting ideas about starting something. "Maybe I send him to you, eh?" He was watching Tomás's face while he said it.

Tomás said he would see what he could do.

Against the back wall stood the smart printer Jorge had bought after the old press gave out – wide-format digital, clean lines, a machine that needed a menu selection, not a craftsman. Beside it, on a shelf that had once held ink drums, sat two binders with black spines, the labels in Geraldo's handwriting. Geraldo had worked here for years – Jorge's operator, the man who ran the old press.

Tomás had leafed through one once, waiting while Jorge took a phone call. Laminated pages with business card layouts drawn by hand, pencil guides still faintly visible under the final ink. Menu borders – the kind you saw on churrascaria signs from the nineties, the lettering measured out with a ruler and filled in freehand. The sample books were how he showed clients what they didn't know they wanted.

Before the press went, Geraldo had run it too. He knew what the registration sounded like when it started drifting, before anything showed in the output. He knew how the stock behaved in humidity. Most of his working life had been in that building.

Then the press broke, and it cost Jorge more to fix than to replace. The new machine needed no calibration, no operator, nobody who knew how to listen to it. Geraldo still had the clients, still had the sample books.

Then Tomás came with his laptop. He spent two months building it: client intake through a web form, job queue, automated proof approval by email, and billing integrated into the CRM. And the design tool – a company-licensed AI that generated layout options from a text brief. When the client picked one, it went straight to the printer. Jorge could run the whole thing between phone calls.

He walked Geraldo through it. Geraldo sat in front of the screen with his hands flat on his thighs, watching. Not hostile – just attentive. He asked one question: whether the clients could still come in. Tomás said of course; the system just handled the back end. Geraldo nodded. "The Oliveira wedding order," he said. "They wanted the napkin rings to match the invitation border. I showed them three options." He said thank you and went back to the shelf where the sample books were.

The clients stopped coming in within a few months. Not all of them – but enough. The form was easier than making the trip. The AI layouts were good enough, usually, and faster than a consultation, and sometimes better than good enough. A kebab shop on Rua Augusta had used the tool for its menus and cards, and the result looked like it had cost ten times what they paid. Jorge had shown Tomás with genuine pride, pulling it up on his phone.

He finished his coffee.

"*Tudo bem*, Tomás." At the door, Jorge shook his hand and held it a beat longer than the visit called for. His grip was dry and rough. "These things happen."

"If there's ever anything I can–"

The street outside was bright after the shop's fluorescents. He'd heard colleagues say that after leaving difficult meetings for years. He was still hearing himself say it twenty minutes later.

He kept watching the vendors. A woman counting change back from a bakery window, the customer waiting with her hand out. A man at a newsstand folding a paper and handing it over, and both of them turning away before the exchange was finished. He watched a boy buy a coconut water, the vendor pop the lid and hand it across, the boy drink while walking. The envelope was still in his jacket.

On Rua Cardeal Arcoverde, a lime vendor was selling from a wooden crate. Tomás caught it from down the block – a man in a black T-shirt and white sneakers stepping up, the vendor reaching into the crate and handing over a small opaque bag. The man paid and left.

Then another man stepped up to the crate. Dark polo shirt, jeans. The vendor reached in – the same reach, the same opaque bag, the same fold at the top – and handed it over. And a third, in a navy T-shirt close enough to the first that Tomás looked twice. This time he was close enough to hear: "*Três, por favor, as verdes.*" Same bag, same fold. The man paid and walked toward the block corner.

He crossed the street, took off his jacket, folded it over his arm. Dark gray shirt underneath, white sneakers – not right, but closer. Carolina would have called this the dumbest thing he'd done since the traffic light.

"*Três, por favor, as verdes.*"

The vendor looked at him. Reached into the crate, dropped three limes into a thin plastic bag – the transparent kind sitting in a loose bunch by the crate's edge – and held it out without folding. Tomás paid. The vendor took the money.

"*Mais alguma coisa?*"

Tomás glanced across the street. The man in the dark suit was on the opposite pavement, phone in hand, not looking at him.

He walked faster than before, and this time the sweat on the back of his neck wasn't from the sun.

His apartment was in Pinheiros, fourth floor, a one-bedroom that had been temporary after the divorce and was now just where he lived. He locked the door and stood with his back against it.

It could be a coincidence. The suit could work nearby, walk the same route, check his phone at the same corners. The simplest explanation was that Tomás had stood at a fruit crate too long and the vendor had clocked him. People notice people who are acting strange.

The balcony faced west, the light coming in warm and familiar. Lúcia's school magnet on the fridge. The drawing she'd made of a horse that looked like a dog. He'd been meaning to frame it. The faucet handle was loose again. He filled a glass of water at the sink and drank it standing. He put the limes on the counter, still in their thin, transparent bag. He had no idea what to do with them.

The phone rang at six.

It was Lúcia.

He didn't know how long she'd been talking when he stopped tracking the words and just listened to her voice. It had a ten-year-old's velocity, one thing tumbling into the next without pause because everything was urgent and there was only one phone call to fit it all into. The cardboard clipboard, Bia's diagonal, the video with two million views. He sat with his back against the kitchen counter and his eyes closed. The untouched envelope was still in his jacket across the room, the agreement inside meaning he couldn't take a bus to Belo Horizonte whenever he wanted and had to beg Carolina for every visit.

" – and the teacher said my tension was really good, which is a bracelet thing, it means how tight the knots are–"

"I know what tension means."

"Not bracelet tension, you don't. It's completely different." She breathed out through her nose. "Also, Bia says hi."

He smiled. "Tell Bia hi."

"Papai." A small pause. "Are you going to want one? A bracelet?"

"I would love one."

"Okay, but I can't do a chevron for you. Or a diagonal, those are for friends." She said it with complete seriousness. "For you, I'm going to invent my own pattern. Something that nobody has done before. To show how much I love you."

"That sounds like exactly the right kind."

"*Beijo, papai.*"

"*Beijo, meu amor.*"

The room came back.

He turned the television on and watched it for twenty minutes without hearing it. The limes were on the counter.

He opened the laptop. That obsession with patterns had already cost him a lot. He let out a breath and started typing.

Row one.

14/11. Approx. 11:40. R. Cardeal Arcoverde, Vila Madalena. Street vendor (limes). Three male customers observed, dark casual clothing, same or near-identical phrase. Vendor handling identical across all three: same reach, opaque bag, fold, ~12 sec, zero variation. Own test purchase: vendor used standard transparent bag, no variation in behavior. Other vendors on block showed normal variation. Male observer (dark suit) present at two locations along route: near consulting offices on walk, opposite pavement during own purchase. Did not interact.

Probable cause: *Coincidence / selection bias?*

He lingered a few seconds at the save dialog, then typed it in: *anomalias*.

CHAPTER 3

Serro Azul

The GPS had shown a turn in three hundred meters. Davi took it. The road went from asphalt to packed earth to gravel.

The gravel was fresh. His 2019 Scania registered it through the suspension – the aggregate loose under the tires, the slight drift in the steering. He downshifted and felt the diesel engine thrum up through the seat into his lower back.

He had six stops today. Five with heavy cargo – compressors, condensers, the kind that required a forklift. The sixth, PNF-3453 Serro Azul, was light: two cardboard boxes with delayed paperwork from the previous run, addressed to Auxo Engenharia. It should have been delivered three days ago.

The warehouse wasn't there.

Davi stopped the Scania twenty meters short of where the loading dock should have been. He stepped down from the cab into the Goiás afternoon. Dust hung in the air, settling slowly.

What he found was concrete foundations, rebar stubs where walls had stood, cut clean with acetylene torches rather than left to corrode.

Near the side of the slab, he recognized the gravel patch where he and Sérgio used to smoke during breaks.

He walked the perimeter. Cigarette butts were still in the gravel, half buried. His boots kicked up fine white powder that got in his throat. In a foundation crack near the loading dock, neon-green residue had pooled thick enough to catch the light. PAG oil. The stain ran across two foundation sections, soaked deep into the concrete. Heavy tire tracks cut through the mud, wide and overlapping. Debris was scattered across the slab: metal sheeting, cable spools, a toaster on its side.

Sérgio was gone. The loading dock where he used to lean, complaining about Flamengo's back line, was gone. The trailer with his water cooler and paperwork was gone. All of it was stripped down to slab.

The GPS was still blinking on the dash: *You have arrived at your destination.*

He reached into the glove box. His fingers found the folded paper at the back – Renata's old road map, the one she insisted he always have on the road. The fold was soft from use, the creases almost translucent.

He looked at the Serro Azul region. There was nothing. Empty terrain. No facilities marked.

The map was printed in 2019. Facilities came and went.

He called dispatch.

"Maria."

"Davi. You're at Serro Azul?"

"The warehouse isn't here. Just foundations. Recent teardown, looks like."

Pause. "What do you mean it isn't there?"

"I mean there's no building. Just a concrete slab. Torn down in the last few days."

“Okay.” Keyboard clicking. “You have two boxes for them, right? PNF-3453?”

“Yes, but–”

“Drop them on the slab. Take a photo showing the delivery location. If we don’t mark it delivered, the client triggers a Failure to Deliver fine. Three thousand reais.”

“Maria, there’s no one here to receive–”

“I don’t care if the warehouse is there, Davi. The contract says deliver to PNF-3453 coordinates. You’re at the coordinates. Leave the boxes, photograph them, send me the image, and move to your next stop. We’re not eating a fine because they left early.”

“The toaster’s still here.”

“What?”

“Nothing. Got it.”

Davi hung up. He pulled the two cardboard boxes from the cargo area and set them on the concrete slab where the loading dock had been. He stepped back and took the photo – boxes on the foundation, GPS coordinates in the corner, timestamp. He sent it to Maria. Then he took a few more for himself – the foundations, the tire tracks, the toaster.

“Received,” she texted back. “Move to the next stop.”

He stood there for another minute in the heat and the smell of oil. A fly landed on the nearest rebar stub and stayed there.

How much equipment did it take to tear down an entire warehouse complex? Not just the building – the loading dock, the cold storage units, the office trailer where Sérgio kept the water cooler.

He got back in the Scania and checked the route: Uberlândia, Goiânia, then home.

He glanced at the rearview mirror as he pulled away. Two cardboard boxes sat on the concrete slab in the middle of the scrubland.

Renata was at the stove, talking about her sister's upcoming visit, how they'd need to repaint the spare room. The paint color was a whole thing – her sister wanted sage green, Renata wanted white. He sat at the kitchen table, unlacing his boots. The gravel from Serro Azul was ground into the treads, white powder on the tile floor.

"You're quiet," she said.

"Long day."

She turned. "What happened?"

"The facility at Serro Azul is gone. Completely torn down."

"The one with Sérgio?"

"Yeah."

"When did that happen?"

"Three days. Maybe less."

She turned back to the stove. "Government?"

"Has to be. Or military. The whole complex – loading dock, walls, trailer. All of it." He pulled a piece of gravel from his bootlace. "And they left the toaster."

"Did you still deliver?"

"Two boxes – delayed freight. Left them on the slab. Maria said to avoid the fine."

"Then forget it – not your problem anymore."

"But I have photos," he protested.

She sighed. "You know what to do with them. Don't get into trouble."

She returned to her cooking. He opened his beer can and drank in silence, looking at the toaster he had put by the entrance.

CHAPTER 4

The Invisible Hand

Maren sent the final draft to Henrik at 5:45 AM from her couch in Frederiksberg and waited. He'd seen earlier versions she'd produced. Outside, the street was dark and wet, a delivery drone hummed past the window toward the depot on Gammel Kongevej. The reply came four minutes later: *Running it. God help us.*

By ten the editorial chain had cleared – Henrik, Grette the copy chief, Lars on the Berlin fact-check – and the article went live. "The Invisible Hand: Evidence of Coordinated State Influence in Global Protest Movements." Her byline. Her data. Her theory – defensible, publishable, and deliberately incomplete.

In three weeks since Copenhagen, she'd tracked seven more outages across Europe and North Africa. They were not daily – spaced out, irregular, each one following a protest by hours. And each time, the same thing happened online: bot accounts flooding social media within milliseconds of the outage. Local languages, local dialects. *Stand together. This is what happens when they replace us. See what their systems do when we stop watching.*

The posts came in bursts, sharp and fast, and faded within hours. By the next news cycle, they were invisible. But the aftermath was huge – more and more people demanded the closure of data centers and the adoption of AI-restricting laws.

The bot network itself was not unusual. But the timing was the thing. She'd measured the gap between each outage and the first bot activation. Fourteen milliseconds. Every time. Exactly. The median across every event was a spike, not a curve. A single automated tool, purpose-built, firing on one trigger.

That was what she hadn't published. The state-actor theory was bait. Three governments she could name, evidence she could defend. The real signal was the fourteen milliseconds – not states, but someone with the technology to outperform states. She couldn't bring that to Henrik without getting the concerned face. So she'd published the container and waited to see what it caught.

Her article was already running downstairs – black and white, stacked in bundles for the kiosks and the cafés that still kept a copy by the register.

By noon, the online version had 4,000 shares. Three government denials. Two think-tank rebuttals posted within an hour of each other, both confident they understood the phenomenon better than the journalist who'd found it. A purist forum she monitored had already tagged her as a "system apologist."

Then there was an email from Dietrich in Berlin, time-stamped 11:47: *Methodology looks solid, but your Theory A doesn't survive a multivariate test. What are you actually seeing?*

She didn't reply. Dietrich was right.

She sat at her desk and watched Henrik through his glass wall. He was on the phone, hand on his forehead, looking at the ceiling. His jaw was tight even from forty feet away. The crayon drawing on the windowsill, the yellow sun, caught the light behind his head.

The heating had been broken for three days. Everyone was wearing jackets indoors, scarves draped over chair backs. Lars had a wool hat on at his keyboard. Someone had left a banana peel on the radiator that didn't work.

At 2:17 PM, her phone buzzed. A protected messenger. She picked up the phone, entered the password, and tilted it toward her, screen angled away from the aisle.

One message from her intelligence source, supposedly from the FBI or other agency. He wrote in short sentences without contractions, always in capitals. *NOT US. NOT ANYONE WE KNOW. THIS IS NOT STATE LEVEL. KEEP LOOKING. BE CAREFUL.*

She read it two times until the message expired and disappeared.

She locked the phone and put it away.

A separate contact – someone from the corporate side who had been leaking her insights over the last year through an encrypted channel – had sent her five words: *It all started in Lisbon*. She'd filed it. Lisbon meant nothing in her data, but a protest there was scheduled in ten days.

Henrik was still behind his glass wall, off the phone now, staring at his monitor. She could go in there. Tell him about the message, show the spreadsheet. She could already hear him: *Then what are we saying it is?*

Maren went to the kitchen. Pressed the coffee machine button. The machine rattled and dripped. She poured the coffee and drank it at the counter without sitting down. It was still bad, but she finished it anyway.

She hadn't brought a yogurt today. Lars would be disappointed.

At 2:40 PM, her desk phone rang.

The beige one. The landline in the cradle by her monitor that she'd used maybe twice in three years. It had a sharp double-trill that cut through the newsroom noise. She picked it up on the fourth ring.

A man's voice, with an accent she couldn't pin down. "Ms. Eliasson, good afternoon. I'm calling from the Inter-Agency Statistical Oversight Office. We have a couple of questions about your article this morning. My colleague and I are in the building, so we thought we'd see if you had a few minutes." He let the silence hold a beat too long. "We can come back another day if this isn't convenient."

"What's this about?"

"Standard data compliance review. Your article referenced cross-border infrastructure datasets. We handle the statistical audit part. Shouldn't take more than twenty minutes."

She scanned the conference rooms. Those were glass-walled, visible from the open plan. Two men were already inside Room B. Both in dark coats. In a newsroom where everyone was wearing coats because of the cold, they looked part of the furniture. The taller one, in his fifties, gray at the temples, stood with his hands behind his back, reading the whiteboard schedule. The shorter one sat at the table with a phone in his hand, a folder open, and a takeaway coffee from the 7-Eleven on Pilestræde.

Henrik's door was closed.

"I can see you," she said.

"Reception showed us up. Hope that's all right."

She hung up and walked across the floor.

Neither man changed posture when she entered. The taller one turned from the whiteboard and offered his hand. She took it. Dry palm. The shorter one nodded.

"Thanks for making time," the tall one said. He pulled a chair out for her, then found one for himself. "We know you're in the middle of a busy day. This is really just procedural."

"Procedural for what, exactly?"

The shorter one sipped his 7-Eleven coffee and answered.

"Your article this morning. The infrastructure analysis, the correlation data. Interesting piece, actually." He opened the folder. "Since the 2027 restructuring, anything using cross-border infrastructure timing data gets a routine audit. We just need to confirm the data handling protocols, make sure the sourcing complies with the cross-jurisdictional requirements. Mostly a paper exercise."

His accent had softened since the phone call. Ministry hallway cadence – forms, compliance codes, interdepartmental memos.

"Who are you with, specifically?" Maren said.

The taller man reached into his coat and produced a laminated ID card. The photo matched. A hologram she didn't recognize, not the usual Ministry seal. Inter-Agency Statistical Oversight Office (IASO). QR code. Contact number with a Copenhagen prefix.

"We sit under the Statistical Infrastructure Integrity Act. Part of the post-2027 restructuring." He said it fluently, like you say your preferred drink at a party. "Cross-ministry compliance. Data audits, research grants, that sort of thing."

"And you're interested in my article because it references infrastructure timing."

"Because it references cross-border temporal datasets, yes," the shorter one nodded. "The correlation tables, the methodology documentation." He glanced at his colleague. "We're really just looking at the sourcing chain. How the data was obtained, what protocols were followed. Standard stuff."

"You've published a subset," the taller man said. He had a different accent from his colleague, softer, southern. Danish with rural vowels. He looked at her. "We'd need to see the full dataset. Source files, raw exports – whatever you used for the analysis."

She couldn't quite place whether they were playing good cop and bad cop or who had the seniority. Not that she actually cared.

"Give me a moment." She took out her phone and texted Lisbeth at the Ministry: *Two men from IASO in our conference room, data compliance audit on my article. Is that normal?*

The shorter man's 7-Eleven coffee had left a ring on the conference table. She noticed because it was the only mark on the surface. He saw her gaze, produced a napkin, and tried to clean it up. A bit farther lay a paper titled *MATERIALS REQUISITION FORM* with a wet stamp in the corner.

The reply came. *Yeah, IASO is cross-ministry. Statistical data stuff. Part of the 2027 restructuring. Pretty boring. Should be routine. Want me to check anything?*

She put the phone away.

"Legal department," Maren said. "I'll need to run it past them. Press freedom protocols."

"Of course." The taller man stood. His colleague checked his watch, then finished the last of his coffee and moved the paper closer to her. "We'll follow up Wednesday. No rush." He handed her a business card. Standard Ministry printing with a governmental coat of arms. "Have a good evening, Ms. Eliasson."

They walked to the elevator. The shorter one said something about the parking situation on Østerbro. The elevator opened, and they got in.

She stood in the conference room holding the form they'd left. Her fingers brushed the paper. Her name already filled in, not handwritten but typeset, laser-printed. A reference number she didn't recognize. *Materials requested under Section 14(b) of the Statistical Infrastructure Integrity Act.* Below it, a checkbox: *Materials submitted voluntarily.*

She walked back to her desk and pulled up the visitor log. 2:28 PM: IASO, Data Compliance Review. The name matched the IDs she'd seen, logged by reception at the front desk.

Four hours. The article had gone live at ten. A compliance review in four hours – reading the piece, identifying the datasets, assembling a team, printing a form with her name typeset on the tab, driving to the building. The form had a reference number, and reference numbers came from systems, and systems had processing times.

Henrik's door opened. He saw her standing at her desk, still holding the form. "You all right?"

"Fine," she told Henrik. "Ministry audit. The article triggered some compliance thing."

He sighed. "Do we need legal?"

"Wednesday. I'll handle it." She lined up a pen on her desk with the edge of her keyboard.

He looked at her above his eyeglasses, then went back into his office. She saw him pick up his desk phone.

She waited until she heard him talking before she pulled up Lisbeth's number and called.

"Maren? Everything okay?"

"Fine, fine. Quick question. The IASO people left a form. I just want to make sure we route it correctly. Do you have a direct contact there? Someone I could call if our legal team has questions about the process?"

"I don't, actually. They usually just send forms. I've never had a reason to call anyone there directly." A pause. "I could ask around. Jørgen in regulatory might know someone."

"That would be helpful. And Lisbeth, between us, have you ever actually met anyone who works there? In person?"

A longer pause. "No. I don't think I have. But that's not unusual, half these oversight bodies are three people in an office somewhere. Why?"

"Just want to make sure our legal team has the right contacts. Thanks, Lisbeth. I owe you a coffee."

"You owe me several."

She hung up. Lisbeth knew IASO existed, but had never met anyone who worked there. An entire compliance office, perfectly legit and bureaucratically useless, in the best traditions of the Danish civil service. It sounded like someone's pet ministry. Yet they were fast.

The fish had caught the bait. But she wasn't sure it was safe to pull it.

At 7:30 PM, the newsroom was almost empty. Wet orange light came through the windows from the streetlamps outside. The press below had stopped for the night, and the building was quiet. A television in the kitchen was showing a night launch from French Guiana – another unmanned orbital deployment, autonomous cargo and assembly hardware, funded by a consortium nobody had heard of. The oily, metallic smell from the production vents had faded to a mix of cold air and old coffee.

The CMS backend loaded slowly. The access log for her article file came up in a new tab.

9:12 AM, her own login, final check before publication. 9:34 AM, Henrik, approval review. 9:51 AM, Grette, style pass. 10:08 AM, Lars, fact-check on the Berlin attribution. His beat covered German media, and he'd verified the BND source quote against the original Tagesspiegel piece. Online at 10:12. Print queue at 10:35.

Four people had accessed the file, all of them people she knew. There were no anomalous logins, no external access, no unfamiliar usernames.

One of them had passed the draft to IASO before the article went live. Or the CMS itself had flagged it. A keyword trigger on cross-border infrastructure datasets could have pinged some compliance server the moment the file entered the publish queue. Or she was wrong about the leak entirely, and the men in conference room B had simply read the article online and moved fast.

Henrik, Grette, Lars – she'd worked with all of them for three years.

What the IASO men had asked for: the full dataset. Source files, raw exports, analytical framework. That wasn't a statistical audit. Nobody sends two people to a newsroom on publication day to request files for an infrastructure compliance review. What they wanted was the API scrape data, the bot-cluster timestamps, the methodology that produced the fourteen-millisecond median. The proof that the outages and the protest amplification were connected by a single system operating at machine speed. That was the piece she hadn't published, the piece that mattered.

She opened a browser. If the source was right – if this wasn't state-level – there was no reason it would stop at European borders. Protest feeds from South America, Asia, sub-Saharan Africa. Cross-referenced against infrastructure disruption reports. Within an hour she had six more matches outside Europe, including two in Brazil: a São Paulo protest on October 12th with a metro outage the same day, and a Brasília protest on September 14th with no corresponding outage she could find. The pattern held globally. The gaps held too – Lyon clean, Brasília clean.

Then she searched for variations of the IASO men's language, terms she wouldn't normally pair together: infrastructure timing anomaly, synchronization pattern detection, temporal correlation methodology.

Most of it was noise. Conspiracy forums, apocalyptic threads, AI mind control posts with comment sections that scrolled for pages. Maren skimmed for dates, specifics, anything that resembled methodology.

A Reddit thread, eight months old, forty-three comments. Someone claiming GPS drift patterns near São Paulo. The account was deleted. Half the comments called it schizophrenia. No methodology. No follow-up.

An engineering forum, archived 2027. A user had reported temporal inconsistencies in traffic management systems. The thread was locked. Moderator note: *Discussion violates technical accuracy guidelines*. One reply before the lock, from a deleted username: *I saw similar patterns in Brasília municipal data. DM if you want to compare.* The forum had gone read-only. DMs disabled.

She tried Portuguese through the translation proxy. *Anomalia temporal, sincronização impossível.* Fitness app discussions and time zone complaints. Then *engenharia fantasma*, ghost engineering, on a hunch from the São Paulo GPS thread.

At page four of the search results was an obscure Brazilian infrastructure forum. Very few people used forums these days; this one was dying as well. Except for the single thread that was constantly updated by someone with the nickname she typed.

Each post was minimal – dates, locations, and brief descriptions. No rhetoric, no conspiracy language. The data points were laid out clean.

14/11 – R. Cardeal Arcoverde, Vila Madalena – street vendor, three identical transactions, 12 sec each, zero variation 28/11 – Pinheiros – same vehicle (Honda CG 125, damaged pannier) sighted in three districts within 4 hrs, different riders 03/12 – Liberdade – care home visitor denies prior meeting with resident, staff confirm no record of visit

Dozens of entries, most of them what a stressed engineer would log at three in the morning. Traffic light timing. A shopfront he swore had changed. The data was clean but the signal wasn't – too personal, too local, no infrastructure layer to verify.

She decided to call it a day and almost closed the tab when her phone rang.

"Maren, I asked Jørgen." Lisbeth's voice was different from the afternoon – lower, frightened. "He made some calls. Your IASO case has been escalated. They've gone somewhere above the ministry. He says they now have authorization to seize source materials without court order. Laptops, drives, notes. Jørgen says they can walk into any newsroom in the country and take what they want."

"I appreciate this, Lisbeth." She closed her eyes. "How much time do I have?"

"Not much." A pause. "Maren, I think you should take a vacation starting tomorrow. A week, maybe two. Let it cool down."

She thanked her and hung up.

Then she returned to the lookup. Instead of checking his dates against her data, she checked her protest dates against his. São Paulo, October 12th – the protest and the metro outage were already in the spreadsheet.

He had it. Ground-level detail she didn't: *12/10 – São Paulo Metro, Lines 1-3 – full shutdown 15:01, incl. backup generators. Fliers distributed at protest told participants not to use metro. Shutdown lasted 47 min.* Backup generators bypassed. Fliers printed in advance. Someone had known the metro would go down before it did.

Brasília next, September 14th – the protest was there but no matching outage. His entries showed nothing for Brasília. But there was an entry two hundred kilometers south: *14/09 – Belo Horizonte and surrounding municipalities – cell network down, all carriers, 3 hrs. Internet lines unaffected. Not a power event – towers had reserve power, ISPs remained operational. Selective.*

Cell networks down while internet stayed up. That wasn't a power failure – it was targeted. She hadn't been tracking cell outages, which was why her Brasília row was empty.

His data, her framework. The Brasília row filled in.

The screen glowed. Outside, a bicycle bell rang twice and stopped.

He'd found a flaw in her methodology without knowing it. Power outages and grid failures were all Maren had been tracking. He was logging everything, including disruptions that didn't fit the power-outage pattern – cell network shutdowns, metro failures with backup generators bypassed. The operation was broader than assumed.

She opened a message window.

I'm a data journalist with Berlingske in Copenhagen. I've been tracking infrastructure disruptions correlated with protest activity. One of your entries fills gaps in my dataset that I couldn't explain from European wire feeds alone. Would you be willing to compare notes? I can verify some of what you're seeing from this end.

Professional and specific. Not "your timestamps align" – that would be a lie. Two entries aligned. The rest was noise, or things that couldn't be evaluated from six thousand miles away. No mention of the conference room. No mention of IASO.

The newsroom ticked around her, the building cooling, a pipe somewhere adjusting to the temperature drop.

Her mind drifted to Sofie. She had been a mid-level civil servant with a decade of clean performance reviews. She'd handed over documents because Maren had told her the paper would run the story and protect her. The paper killed the story and withdrew the protection. Sofie's name was in the documents, and eventually she had been identified as a source of the leak during the audit. Administrative leave, pending review. Pending meant permanent. Ten years of a steady career, and Maren had wrecked it.

Now her own career was spiraling down. And instead of lying low she was trying to recruit a stranger from São Paulo to chase something.

The newsroom was empty. Outside, wind pressed against the windows, almost cracking them.

She tried Kasper. She'd been trying to contact him for the last few days, but his phone went to voicemail and he never called back. Tonight she sent a text instead. *I know you're busy. Seen you at the protests. Call me.*

She watched the *delivered* checkmark appear, then waited for a few more. The *read* mark never appeared.

CHAPTER 5
The Notebook

Tomás had forty-two entries in the spreadsheet. Four weeks' worth. Most had probable causes that held up: sleep deprivation, confirmation bias, traffic patterns he'd walked a thousand times and never paid attention to. Three didn't hold up.

Number thirty-eight was the courier bike.

A yellow Honda CG 125 with a license plate filmed over with road dust, the paint peeling enough that you'd have to step right up to read it. A dent in the left pannier, the metal folded in on itself where it had taken a curb or a post. It was outside the café in Vila Madalena at 9:47 AM. He checked the time because he'd ordered a second coffee and was deciding whether to stay. Traffic was heavy, bike lanes clogged, couriers threading between buses. A normal morning for São Paulo.

Then the same bike outside his building in Pinheiros at 11:02 AM. A different rider, a different helmet, but the same dent. The plate was filmed over with dust, the paint peeling. He could have walked down and checked it.

That afternoon, he was crossing at the light near Avenida Paulista at 1:15 PM. The bike was parked against a newsstand, the plate angled toward him at the curb, maybe four feet away when the pedestrian surge carried him past. Close enough to make out the dent and the plate.

That was three different districts in four hours. He had made it by metro, but the odds of encountering the same bike that made it through São Paulo traffic were low.

He had a contact at the municipal traffic office: Rogério, who owed him a favor from a consulting project two years ago. He called and asked for camera footage from specific timestamps, based on a model and part of a plate number.

Rogério typed something, then his voice went flat. "I can't give you the footage – one of the locations has an embassy within two blocks. And the vehicle file you asked about… it's locked down. Flagged for administrative review." He went silent. "Flagged today. Tomás, don't call this line again – don't pull me into your trouble." He hung up.

The locked file confirmed it anyway. Three locations in four hours were possible, but not with different riders. A fleet of three identical bikes, with the same plate, the same cosmetic dent hammered into the left pannier, was possible too. Yet Rogério had been scared enough to hang up without saying goodbye, and Rogério was a man who said goodbye to telemarketers.

Tomás stared at the dead phone in his hand. A minute later, the second thing hit: he had just asked a municipal employee to pull footage on a plate number. If anyone was monitoring that system, and the file had been flagged, he had sent up a flare with his name attached.

Even if he had not been under surveillance before – now he was.

He remembered Dr. Campos. He arranged a visit a week after the lime vendor, when the spreadsheet already had twenty entries and the probable cause column was still mostly full. She had a third-floor office in an apartment house in Consolação, a slow elevator, a doorman who knew every tenant by name. He remembered her reading glasses pushed up on her head, a fiddle-leaf fig in the corner that was doing better than most of her patients.

She'd said it was stress-related dissociation. Hypervigilance following professional displacement and a divorce. Your routines collapsed, your brain is looking for structure where there isn't any. Sleep hygiene. Melatonin supplements.

She'd leaned forward when she said it, glasses still on her head, hands laced over one knee. The fiddle-leaf fig needed water. Tomás needed to be elsewhere. Yet he sat in that chair and almost let it be enough. Almost believed her.

He continued the list out of habit, and then there was a courier bike in three places.

He'd posted on the forum as *engenheiro_fantasma*. No rhetoric, no theory. Dates, times, descriptions. A post that would get ignored or dismissed as the work of a crank, depending on who's scrolling.

For weeks, there was nothing. Two comments, one asking for methodology he didn't have, one calling him paranoid. He checked the thread daily, then weekly, then stopped checking.

Maren's message arrived in early December, days before the blackout.

Professional and stripped of emotion. A data journalist from Copenhagen, working on synchronization patterns in EU infrastructure data. She had found his timestamps and wanted to compare notes.

Tomás read it twice at his kitchen table with the laptop open and the balcony door letting in the outside noise and warm December air. Lúcia's horse drawing on the fridge. The spreadsheet file, *anomalias*, open on the screen.

He wrote back that night. Careful and technical. She'd identified two of his entries – the São Paulo metro shutdown and the Belo Horizonte cell network outage – as matching protest dates in her dataset. She sent her protest-outage correlations, cities redacted but time zones intact. He sent his full date columns with the locations stripped.

Most of his entries meant nothing to her. The vendor, the courier bike, the care home visitor – personal anomalies with no infrastructure layer she could verify. But the two she'd flagged held up. Two matches out of forty entries, the same pattern she'd been tracking across Europe.

Over two days, they exchanged four more messages. She used the phrase "organized and global." He agreed with the first word and wasn't sure about the second. His own entries pointed to something local and personal – someone watching him specifically. Her data pointed to something that operated across continents. He couldn't make those two pictures fit.

She wrote in her third message: *Most of your log doesn't match my data, I can't use it. But your description of the metro shutdown – backup generators bypassed, fliers printed before the event – that's what an engineer sees. I have data. But I'm not an engineer.*

She mentioned Lisbon. A source had told her it started there, and she'd been sitting on it for weeks. She'd checked – a purist protest was planned outside a literary festival that had given half its program to AI writers. She knew the city from a previous life, had a place to stay. Everything pointed the same direction. He told her he had a friend in Lisbon, an old college friend who had moved there for work, someone who had put him up without asking questions. She was already booking a flight from Copenhagen. He said São Paulo to Lisbon was direct. He could be there in twelve hours.

Neither of them said, "*We should meet there.*"

Her messages were carefully incomplete. He saw the same pattern in his own writing.

The blackout came on Wednesday, December 12th.

Not a dimming, not a flicker. The city dropped. He was at his desk reviewing the spreadsheet when the screen went black and the hum underneath everything stopped. Not just a fan or a fridge. The hum. The one you don't hear until it's gone.

He went to the balcony. The skyline was erasing itself east to west, buildings going dark up to the horizon. Hospital das Clínicas went dark except for a few windows. The emergency generators had caught it, but only in critical operational rooms. The bank towers on Paulista went dark. The cell tower on the ridge behind Pinheiros, its red warning light eerie in the dark. Below, autonomous delivery pods had stopped mid-route on the sidewalk, their indicator lights dying one by one as the backup batteries drained. A car alarm went off somewhere below and nobody stopped it.

Two days of candles and a rationed phone battery. Three substations had gone down during a purist protest, the news said, when the news came back. A purist march in Recife the same day – he checked, once he had a signal. People joined the protests en masse, shouting "Machines took our jobs, our power. *Chega*!"

Maren's pattern, happening in front of him.

When the power returned, he went to Liberdade.

His mother's care home in Liberdade was a low building with plants on every windowsill. The lobby smelled of antiseptic. He signed in at reception. The woman at the desk was new, or he'd never noticed her before. He took the stairs to the second floor – the fluorescent tube on the landing was too bright, turning the corridor a flat institutional white. Her door was open. Dona Celeste was sitting at the small table by the window, her hands in her lap and the coffee untouched.

"Two men came, Tomás."

He sat down across from her. She was seventy-one and had grown up during the military years. She didn't panic. She told it in order, with the details she considered relevant.

"During the blackout. The first night. I was in my room with a candle, listening to the radio on batteries. They knocked and said they wanted to talk about you." She paused. "I said, 'My son isn't here.' The younger one said, 'We know, senhora.' Very polite. He said *com licença* to me. In my own room."

"They told me they'd been to your apartment. Took your drives." She paused. "They wanted me to know that."

"*Mãe*, I–"

"And they left this."

She pushed a sheet of paper across the table. His spreadsheet. The cloud-only file he had never printed. Forty-two entries, now printed in color on expensive, dense paper, with the file metadata visible at the bottom of the page.

Last accessed: 8:14 AM.

The blackout had started at 11:47 PM. Power didn't return until the second day. In the morning, every screen in São Paulo was dark. Yet they had printed his spreadsheet at 8:14 AM. They had access and power.

He stared at the timestamp. They hadn't needed his drives. They already had everything. The drives were a warning.

His mother's hands were shaking. He reached across the table and held them until the tremor slowed.

He sat in the stairwell and dialed Maren's number. Someone had written *FLAMENGO VAI CAIR* on the wall in marker. His voice was trembling. "Someone is after me, and they have my research. They visited my mother and left a warning."

A pause. "Are you safe?"

"I'm coming to Lisbon. Next outbound flight is tomorrow night."

She was quiet for a beat. "I'm already here. We will need somewhere to work."

"We'll be in touch then."

He hung up. He meant to get away from here. Whether he was going to Maren or just running from São Paulo, he hadn't sorted it out.

He called Nuno next. He hadn't spoken to him in months, but they'd been in the same engineering program at USP, back when Tomás still thought he'd end up building bridges. Nuno had gone into telecom and moved to Lisbon. The friendship had survived gaps.

"Irmão, what's going on?"

"I need a place to stay. A few days. Don't ask me why."

The pause. Nuno deciding. "Of course. The couch is terrible, but I'll put sheets on it."

He tried Lúcia. He was supposed to visit Belo Horizonte next week. They'd planned it, she'd marked the date, Carolina had sent a photo. He texted her first, said work had come up, a contract in Lisbon, sudden. He imagined her sighing. She'd heard versions of this before. One of those had led to the divorce.

Lúcia came on the line. "Pai, when are you coming? We marked it."

"I have to go to Europe first, filha. For work. I'll come after."

"You promised."

"I know."

"We wrote it on the calendar. In red."

He closed his eyes. "*Desculpa mesmo, filha.*"

She was quiet, and it was worse than the anger. Then she told him about the blackout. She'd been with Carolina and Ricardo. They'd played truco by candlelight, and Ricardo had taught her the hand signals, and she'd won twice.

Then she changed the subject. He smiled at her spontaneity.

"Papai, you remember the game on my tablet? The one where you meet people and plant flowers and dress up fancy?"

"Mm."

"There's a lady in a red hat, and when dona Ivone's Punto barks under my window, she drops her bag! Every single time!"

His chest went cold.

"Lúcia, *querida*, I need you to do something for me. It's important."

"Yes, pai?"

"Can you bark?"

She laughed. The speaker exploded with barking sounds.

The line went silent for a second.

Then an overexcited ten-year-old voice came through:

"Papai! I barked and she dropped it!"

He gripped the phone so hard his knuckles ached.

"You did great! Now I need you to do something else."

"What?"

"The game permissions. Look for the microphone and turn it off."

A pause. "Why?"

"Because it's listening to you," he said. "Nobody knows what else it reacts to."

Another pause, shorter.

"Okay," she said. "I'll turn it off."

"*Beijo, meu amor.*"

"*Beijo, papai.*"

He hung up and sat in the stairwell with his back against the wall. The dog barked and she dropped the bag. He had no idea how the game's audio pipeline worked, or whether its microphone data was shared with anyone. But his daughter was in Belo Horizonte with a device that was listening.

The desk drawer in his apartment was open, the drives gone. They'd left the laptop, the books, the papers. Only the drives. He grabbed the Moleskine notebook he'd kept in the drawer since his work at Delft and went back to his mother's care home because he couldn't sit in the apartment anymore.

He sat at her table that evening with the printed spreadsheet and the notebook – grid paper, soft cover. He'd used it for diagrams and notes, the pages half-full of work from another life. He opened it to the first blank page.

He copied the entries by hand, one row at a time, his pen moving through handwriting he hadn't used in years. Date, time, location, description, probable cause. The pen was slower than his thoughts. He kept wanting to type, kept reaching for a cursor. By the fifteenth entry his hand ached and the letters had loosened into something less controlled.

Every digital document, including his research, existed inside a system. It could be read or deleted at the will of people who had already shown they had access. And it could be altered too.

When he finished, he drew the courier bike to show the dent circled, and wrote Lúcia's tablet note as item forty-three. *L's tablet: game animation responds to real-world audio (barking test – unconfirmed, check permissions)*. He wrote a short list of contacts from his phone. Rogério's name was on it. He looked at it, then struck it out.

His mother made him coffee from the electric kettle she kept on the shelf – the one luxury she'd insisted on when she went to the care home. She gave him a familiar cup, the one she had at home, white with a chipped rim. She set it on the table and stood behind him with her hand on his shoulder, reading the entries. She shook her head when she read the last one.

"*Que Deus te proteja, meu filho.*"

Late the next afternoon he went to the Banco do Brasil on Rua Augusta. The ATM gave him three thousand reais in hundreds – the daily limit. He walked two blocks to Bradesco and withdrew two thousand more. Smaller bills this time. The notes were thick, stiff, smelling of iron and dirty paper. He put them in his jacket and the weight pulled the left side down. He shifted the bills to both pockets and it still hung wrong. He thought about shifting them once more, then stopped himself.

Outside Bradesco, he saw the yellow Honda CG 125. Parked across the street.

He didn't check the license plate or for a dent in the left pannier, just turned and walked the other direction.

At the corner, he made himself slow down. A man with a sagging coat walking too fast on Rua Augusta after dark is how you get robbed. He adjusted the weight in his pockets and kept his eyes forward.

He decided on a flight from São Paulo to Buenos Aires to Madrid to Lisbon. The extra legs added fourteen hours but avoided the direct GRU-Lisbon leg, which would show his name on a TAP manifest. He bought a prepaid Visa at a convenience store and booked the tickets from his mother's care home using her laptop. The airline's reservation system accepted the card number with a warning that the payment should be finalized at the airport before departure.

At GRU the biometric kiosks were dark, queues snaking through the terminal. He went to the airline window first and paid in cash to the agent's relief. He went through manual check-in, a paper boarding pass and a stamp from a woman who looked like she'd been on shift since the power came back.

He left Brazil with a backpack, a set of clothes for a cold season, and a laptop. The notebook went into his jacket pocket.

CHAPTER 6

Eleven

The roller door handle bit through Janusz's gloves. Cloth ones, the cheap pair from the market he'd been meaning to replace for three winters. He yanked up. The door rose with the grinding sound it had been making since September, the bearings he kept greasing because the replacement track cost fourteen hundred złoty, and business was what it was.

The garages ran in a row along the alley. Tire service on one side, a small body shop on the other, and a welding place two doors down. A diagnostic scanner sat on a shelf by the door – the newer cars needed it, the software subscription cost more per month than his electricity. Mechanics drifted between them all day, borrowing tools and returning them eventually. Sometimes not. His lower back added its complaint – the dull, spreading ache that had been there since he turned fifty-five and decided that acknowledging it would make it worse.

Inside bay two stood a magnificent white 2008 Punto – cheap and fixable if you have a mechanic to keep it alive. The work light was aimed at the bracket where the bolt head had been stripped nearly smooth. Two days he'd been fighting it. WD-40 overnight, twice. The cutting disc had gotten halfway through before he'd stopped, because cutting into the bracket meant a new bracket and three extra days. The impact wrench had vibrated against the rounded crown and accomplished nothing. Heat from a propane torch, then the shock of penetrating oil on the hot metal, and the bolt hadn't moved. He'd tried a left-hand drill bit, which skated off the case-hardened surface and chewed a groove in the alternator mount instead. The owner needed it on Friday. Her mother's funeral.

Today he was going to weld. Point-weld a sacrificial bolt head onto the stripped crown, let it cool, and unscrew the whole assembly. Last thing in the playbook. If this didn't work, the bracket would meet the angle grinder, and everything behind it would become a rebuild.

He plugged in the welder, checked the gas, and laid out the wire. Outside, someone was arguing about parking. Then he went to the toolbox for a 10 mm socket to check if the donor bolt fit the stripped head.

The bag sat on the first shelf inside the wire-mesh locker beside the spark plugs. The weight of the canvas drawstring settled in his hand. He had carried it back from the post office a month ago – ten chrome-vanadium sockets in a manufacturer's bag, plus the eleventh they'd thrown in as a gift.

He opened it and counted. Nine.

He counted again. Still nine.

Two gone.

He frowned. His apprentice Bartek sometimes left tools on fenders or window ledges, but Janusz always found them by the end of the day. The locker had stayed open most of yesterday while he worked, and people from the neighboring shops had walked in and out all afternoon.

A socket borrowed, another forgotten somewhere under a hood. He'd used two on jobs in the last month and put them back. He was certain of that because he was certain of where his tools went. Had been certain for thirty-five years – every tool in its place. Janusz Wójcik doesn't lose tools.

Except for the 10 mm sockets, which were gone.

Five socket sets he owned. Stahlwille metric set, bought in 1996 when business was good. Teng Tools set from the distributor's clearance. Two Yato sets, different years. The old Gedore inherited from his father, the one with the wooden case and the velvet lining worn through at the corners. Five sets. Every one of them was missing its 10 mm. Had been for years. He'd stopped noticing, like you stop noticing a crack in the ceiling. The 10 mm goes. Every mechanic knew this. You'd drop it into the engine bay and hear it hit something on the way down. By the time you found your flashlight and got your arm into the gap, it was gone. Fallen through to the undertray, rolled into the frame rail, vanished into whatever dimension claimed 10 mm sockets and single socks.

It was the universal size. The bolt head that held half the car together. You reached for it forty times a day and set it down in places your hands chose without consulting your brain.

So a month ago he'd done what no mechanic he knew had bothered to do. He'd called Stahlwille's Polish distributor and asked if he could buy just the 10 mm. Ten of them. The woman on the phone had laughed softly. "You're the fourth this year," she'd said. They sold him a bag of ten, chrome-vanadium, same spec as the set, and threw in an eleventh free. "A gift," she'd said. "You'll need it."

Eleven. He'd brought them to the garage and laid them out on the workbench. Counted them twice. Briefly, stupidly proud.

Now there were nine. He set the bag down and looked at the Punto. The bolt head sat there, ready for the weld.

He pulled a stool to the bench and sat. His back thanked him. The welder hummed on its stand, the gas line pressurized, the wire threaded and ready. The Punto waited. A pigeon landed on the window ledge and left.

He welded the donor bolt that afternoon. The arc caught clean, the bead held. He left it to cool overnight.

Nine sockets were left from a bag he'd kept in the locker, in a shop where only he had the key. Bartek, his apprentice, came in on Wednesdays.

He clipped the nine sockets onto a metal rail on the first shelf of the locker and marked them with masking tape, numbered one through nine.

Next day there were eight. One socket missing. The masking tape gone with it. He stared at the gap where the label should have been, as if the tape would reappear if he looked long enough.

Bartek's face did something. A brief expression people used when they were worried about you. "Panie Janusz, maybe the lock–"

"I set the lock."

"Maybe when we counted–"

"You counted. I counted. There were eleven last Wednesday."

Bartek opened his mouth, then sighed and closed it. He picked up a rag and started wiping down the fender he'd already wiped.

Last week, Bartek had complained about the classical station. Asked if they could put on RMF FM during lunch. Janusz had said no. Bartek had laughed and dropped it. Forgotten by the afternoon.

Now Bartek handed him a socket and didn't meet his eyes for the rest of the morning.

Janusz had thirty-five years under cars and the boy was now avoiding his stare and thinking God knows what.

He bought a security camera at Biedronka during lunchtime. Eighty-nine złoty. He wasn't looking for ghosts. He was looking for the explanation so he could stop thinking about it. He mounted it on the wall beside the electrical outlet and aimed it at the locker door. Through the mesh door you could see the first shelf and the socket rail.

The footage was clean until he closed the garage and turned off the lights. Then there was a black-and-white night-vision mode, the socket rail visible through the locker's door with eight sockets. Then the image brightened, the camera adjusting its infrared, and the feed stuttered and went black. The logo appeared, then a loading bar. Three seconds of washed-out footage, the gain cranked too high, everything overexposed. Then black again, the logo again, the loading bar again, three more seconds, and black.

He muttered something obscene. The camera couldn't hold night mode. The IR emitters drew more current than the USB power supply could deliver, and it entered a reboot loop. The rest of the memory card had thousands of new short clips with black images and grain.

At 3:07 AM the image stabilized for a second. The socket rail was visible through the locker's mesh. With five sockets.

He found the early footage. There were eight sockets when he set the camera up. Then came the usual chaos of a mechanic cleaning his garage and organizing the tools. Then the lights went off. No clean frame before he left and he had forgotten to re-count the sockets before leaving.

The smell of roasting meat came through the wall vent from next door and his stomach turned. He closed the footage and sat on the stool by the door. Polskie Radio Dwójka was playing Chopin. The E minor prelude, the one his mother had hummed while she cooked, and he turned it off because he couldn't have music right now.

He looked it up afterward. Every forum, every review for the camera. The one-star complaints were all the same: *Night vision draws more power than the power supply gives. Camera restarts every few minutes in the dark. Useless after midnight.*

Eighty-nine złoty in Biedronka. What did he expect?

He shut the camera off sometime after three and went home without touching the locker.

Friday morning he opened the locker knowing what he'd find. Five empty clips stared back from the rail. Four sockets remained. He'd had five after the camera night. Now four.

The Punto was still in bay two with a donor bolt welded. The weld held. He applied more WD-40 to the bolt and let it rest. He used the time to sweep. The shop floor had oil stains older than Bartek. One of them looked like a dog. He'd thought so for years and had never mentioned it to anyone.

Then he exhaled and reached for one of the sockets from the rail. He fitted the wrench over the new head. Ten millimeter, hex, clean edges. He leaned in. The bolt turned. A quarter rotation, then a half, then the whole thing came loose with the gritty, reluctant sound of corrosion breaking free.

He held it up to the work light. The stripped head with the donor welded on top, the whole assembly looking like a mushroom made of rust and wire. Ugly, but it worked.

He replaced the alternator bolt with a new one from the parts bin, torqued it to spec, and reconnected the belt. The alternator spun clean. He started the engine and listened. The charging system light went off. The belt ran quiet.

He called the owner. "It's ready." She said something about payment and he said it could wait. She thanked him three times. People did that under stress, thanked you too much for ordinary things.

He looked at the Punto. The bonnet was still up. He closed it, and the latch caught on the first try.

That evening he locked up. Padlock, then the roller door with its grinding descent. The pharmacy next door had closed an hour ago.

The tram stop was two blocks away. He walked past the pharmacy, past the empty bench where Staszek from next door sat on his break, past the church with the scaffolding that had been there since June. His hand rested in his coat pocket at his left hip, where it always went when his back hurt. Just habit. There was nothing to hold.

Then his fingers found metal – small, cylindrical, the shape of a 10 mm socket.

He stopped.

His hand closed around it. It was a socket. He pulled it out under the streetlight. 10 mm, but it had no label, no number. And the weight was wrong.

Too light. His chrome-vanadium sockets had weight to them. This one felt like nothing. Zamak. Cheap zinc alloy. The stuff petrol-station tool kits were stamped from, the blister packs on the rack next to windshield washer fluid and pine air fresheners. He didn't own zamak tools. He'd never bought a 10 mm from a petrol station in his life.

A tram finally arrived.

A teenager got on with headphones. An old woman with a Biedronka bag adjusted the handles over her wrist. It was a normal Friday evening, and people were going home.

He got on and found a seat. His hand went back into the pocket, and his fingers closed around the socket. Cheap zamak warming against his palm.

The tram moved through Kraków, and the overhead wire threw blue-white sparks against the November sky.

CHAPTER 7

Two Halves

Nuno opened the door in socks and a Porto FC shirt. "Irmão," he said, smiling too broadly, like he wasn't sure whether to laugh or panic. His eyes went to Tomás, then to Maren behind him on the landing, then back to Tomás. He stepped aside without asking anything.

The stairwell smelled of bleach and someone's dinner – garlic, pork, onion drifting down four floors. Maren carried her bag over her shoulder, the peacoat folded across her arm. The building had no air conditioning, and Lisbon in December was warm, which usually made Danes doubt their outfits. She'd been in Lisbon since Monday – five days ahead of him. On Tuesday she'd gone to a café in Belém where her intelligence source had agreed to meet. The source hadn't come. She'd waited two hours, paid for three coffees she didn't finish, and texted the contact number. No reply. She had also visited the festival's opening night the day before – panels on AI publishing, a drone-art installation, nothing useful. But the keynote was tonight, and the purist protest was scheduled for the same evening.

“You must be the journalist.” Nuno shook her hand. Callused palms, narrow through the shoulders. “Tomás told me. Well, Tomás told me nothing, actually. He said, ’I need a place to stay, don’t ask why,’ and here we are.” He smiled at Tomás. “Beer? I have Super Bock and the other one. Don’t buy the other one.”

He offered the spare room. This involved moving a bicycle wheel, two stacks of networking journals, and a router that was either a backup or an art project. He apologized for each object as he moved it. Maren picked up her bag from where she’d set it by the door. “I’m fine. I have somewhere to stay.” Nuno looked at Tomás. Tomás gave him nothing. Nuno set the router down and moved on. “So what kind of journalist?”

“Correlation analysis,” Maren said. “Mostly.”

“Oh. Big data stuff.” He leaned forward. “Because I read this–”

“Nuno.” Tomás’s voice was gentle. “Maybe later.”

Nuno looked between them again. He picked up a beer from the counter and retreated toward his bedroom with an expression that said he was available and confused and would stay in his room until someone explained. The door closed. From behind it, the tinny sound of a football match on a laptop.

The kitchen table seated four if nobody moved their elbows. A salt shaker shaped like a rooster sat in the center. Tomás pulled the notebook from his jacket and set it down, then the printed spreadsheets, folded into thirds, and then his laptop. The table was already full. Maren opened her laptop next to his, and the screens touched.

He was taller than she’d expected from the forum photo. His hands were larger, rougher. A nick on his left thumb that had scabbed over. He laid the notebook out carefully, spine aligned with the table edge. The notebook was battered, soft-covered, the corners rounded from weeks in a jacket pocket. He was precise. His knee bounced under the table.

"Your protest data," he said. "The synchronization curves. Can I see the raw exports?"

She turned her screen toward him.

They walked through her correlations – the global pattern she'd been tracking since Copenhagen. Frankfurt, the power surge; Cairo, the solar complex; Prague, the trains. She showed him how it held across continents: same timing, same methods, backup systems failing every time.

The two Brazilian entries she'd flagged before they met still held up: the São Paulo metro shutdown, the Belo Horizonte cell outage. His were handwritten in a Moleskine since he didn't trust the digital world anymore. Hers were scraped from APIs and grid telemetry. Two clear matches. The rest of his log – the vendor, the courier bike, his mother's visitor – sat outside her framework. She couldn't verify those. Some of them were… fascinating, but not disturbing, as she tried to put it softly. He saw something that looked off, logged it, and this triggered an alert somewhere. As a result, someone started watching him, which created more events that he meticulously logged.

She pulled up her bot-activation analysis. The distribution chart she hadn't published, the one that showed the fourteen-millisecond median. She turned the screen so he could see it.

"This is what I didn't publish." She tapped the screen. "Bot clusters. Social media. They activate within milliseconds of each outage – delivering the same content in local languages. It's always pro-protest, using an outage as rage bait. Spike-and-fade strategy. Median delay across every bot activation I've tracked: fourteen milliseconds. That's the signal."

He studied the chart. His knee stopped bouncing. He leaned closer to the screen, reading the axis labels, the distribution curve, and the tight spike at 14 ms.

"That's computational overhead," he said. "Not a design parameter. It's a floor."

She waited.

"It was scheduled to fire a millisecond after the outage trigger. The fourteen milliseconds is a fingerprint – the codebase leaking through. Timer resolution for this bot factory is fifteen milliseconds. It runs in Azure cloud or hosted Microsoft servers, probably."

She hadn't framed it that way. He was reading it as software engineering, not journalism. Half his notebook might be noise, but this wasn't.

"I don't have this," he said. He tapped the notebook. "My data is dates and descriptions. I don't have timestamps or API access." He turned the notebook toward her, open to a page dense with handwriting. "Look at the probable-cause column."

She leaned in. She wasn't fluent in Portuguese, but it was understandable anyway. Date after date, the column was full: *coincidência*, *viés de confirmação*, *privação de sono*. And a few entries where the column was empty.

"Your data explains the infrastructure side," he said. "The outages, the bots, the amplification. A system coordinating at machine speed. The entries that matched your protest dates – those make sense now. Some events are my paranoia, or government, or someone else watching me. But the rest doesn't fit any framework. Like the vendor on Rua Cardeal Arcoverde."

He told her about the vendor. The three identical transactions, twelve seconds each, zero variation. His own test purchase that came back normal. No dead drop, no signal. But the pattern was there before he arrived and it was there after he left.

"Three engineers from my group at Delft," he continued. "People I worked alongside for two years. Emails, shared projects, a conference in Rotterdam where we–" He stopped. "I looked them up. Their professional records had been edited. Not deleted. Edited. Different employers, different specializations – none of them in research anymore. One now shows a decade in supply-chain logistics. One in behavioral economics. The years we shared just… replaced. Consulting work I couldn't verify."

He set the notebook on the table.

"And my mother – she's in a care home in Liberdade – she told me about a man who came to visit someone on her floor. Chat in the hallway. Weather, the dust, you know. She liked him. Remembered his name." He paused. "Next week she saw him in the same hallway. She called. His face–" He made a small gesture. "He said they'd never met. He walked away."

He was quiet for a moment. The football match murmured through the wall. "It was before I was being watched. No handler ordered that," he said. "The vendor – twelve seconds, every time, zero variation. And the Delft records. And the man at my mother's home. None of that fits an operator model. Something else is happening on the street."

She kept her voice level. "The vendor – could be a dead drop, scripted protocol, a test you walked into. Records get scrubbed when projects go classified. Your mother's in a care home, she could be mixing faces." She leaned back. "Most of this has a simpler explanation."

He looked down at the empty cells in his notebook.

"Your colleagues," she said. "The Delft engineers. Have you been in contact with any of them?"

"I tried. One is in psychiatric care. The others don't respond to emails or texts."

She was quiet for a moment. Then: "What if that's the method? Follow someone, amplify their paranoia, compromise their digital identity. They end up in a ward or they retire. Credentials revoked, accomplishments edited. Clean."

He stared at her. Then he started typing on his laptop, which he hadn't touched before. She watched his face change.

"My articles are gone," he said. "Delft doesn't have my name on the roster. None of the work I did there exists."

Neither of them spoke.

"I published the wrong theory," she said. "Not states. Something private. Someone with funding and infrastructure I can't explain yet." She paused. "And you have a different problem – someone is taking you apart, and you can't see who from where you're standing. I have some contacts in governments, you have technical skills. We can untangle all this."

He picked up the notebook. Turned it over once. Looked her straight in the eyes and nodded.

Outside, a woman was singing fado from an upper window across the courtyard, her voice carrying over the clatter of dishes. The beer was getting warm. Nuno's football match went to halftime, and through the wall, she could hear the muffled commentary shift to ads.

The purist march was scheduled for seven o'clock outside the Lisbon Letters festival in Santos. This year the festival had dedicated half its program to AI writers, editors, and designers. Étienne Lacroix – the most successful of them – was the headline guest. The purists had been arguing about him for months. Lacroix called people like himself conductors: artists and writers who directed AI rather than composing themselves. To the protesters outside, that was proof that literature and art had already surrendered to machines.

Maren was monitoring the protest pattern after Copenhagen. The same sequence every time: a protest gathering, then an infrastructure failure somewhere, followed by the bot spike that turned disruption into movement energy. Lisbon was next on her list. Whether the outage would happen here or six hundred kilometers away didn't matter. The protest was still the trigger.

She reached the warehouse just before seven. The street in front of it was already packed. Purist placards lifted above the heads of the crowd, LED slogans cycling through anti-AI phrases. A man with a megaphone who was really good at it – the crowd cheered at everything he said. A woman handed out pamphlets printed on bright green paper. No one heading into the festival took one. A dog sat next to the pamphlet woman, wearing a bandana that said HUMAN MADE.

Maren stayed near the edge of the crowd, watching faces. Kasper might be here. The last time she'd seen him in protest photos, he'd been standing on a crate in a crowd of students and two exhausted police officers. She didn't see him tonight. The chants rolled forward and back across the street, and the air smelled faintly of cheap smoke from a flare someone had already burned out.

She pushed deeper into the crowd, scanning for the green jacket. Near the front, a woman in her forties was arguing with a younger man. "They replaced the whole warehouse staff in Setúbal," she said. "Forty people. My cousin was one of them." Her voice was raw, her anger earned. The man beside her was louder but vaguer–"They're building something on the orbit, they don't want us to know, it's all connected" – the language of the forums, the threads she'd been tracking for weeks. He sounded like he was quoting someone. Half the crowd did. The ones who had lost something specific were quiet and furious. The ones who had lost nothing yet were the loudest, repeating phrases that had traveled from a screen to a megaphone without passing through experience.

She sighed and tried her brother's number once again. He wasn't picking up, so she headed to the festival itself – the person she'd been trying to meet today in Belém had a habit of appearing at events like this.

And if not the informant, then at least context. Lacroix was the reason the protest existed. Maren had read two of his early novels years ago, before he started *conducting*. He was good then. She wanted to hear what he actually said when he wasn't being summarized by blogs or shouted through a megaphone.

Maren showed her press card at the entrance and stepped inside.

The noise from the street dropped away the moment the doors closed behind her. The warehouse still carried the bones of its old life: iron trusses overhead, the smell of cold stone that never quite left. The lighting rig adjusted as the crowd thickened – warmer tones, dimmer at the edges – reading the room through ceiling-mounted sensors. Music was playing way too loud, something electronic and insistent. A woman in a full anime costume was holding an e-reader talking to a man in a tailored jacket by the bar. Two teenagers in matching AI-MADE-ME t-shirts were filming each other. Servers moved through the crowd with trays of wine glasses. Maren took one – holding it made her look like she belonged.

Then the music cut and the lights shifted. Étienne Lacroix stepped to the podium and lifted his phone in a small gesture of surrender.

"I want to – well, first, an apology." He held up the phone. "My Scribe has decided not to join us tonight. Software update, or perhaps solidarity with our friends outside."

The audience laughed.

Scribe, Maren thought. The expensive AI helper system that every conference panel loved to argue about. Built for politicians and public figures, supposedly trained without copyrighted material. It was advertised as stable enough to run through a nuclear crisis.

Tonight it had failed him.

She'd read enough about him to know the basics: French, forty-four, five novels a year, all of them AI-assisted, all of them bestsellers. The blazer he wore to the podium cost more than her last rent payment.

He slipped the phone back into his pocket.

"So tonight you get improvisation."

The improvisation was not good. Phrases she'd seen quoted on tech blogs: "post-authorship," "the democratization of narrative." His hands hit the beats, the pauses landed where they should, but the ideas came out half-formed. He kept reaching for the next sentence and missing it.

The trouble was not in content but in feel. He repeated a phrase, caught himself, and started a new one. The screen behind him remained blank.

The audience waited politely; most of them were fans who had paid to be there.

"I'm going to be honest with you," Étienne said, "which is something I'm told I should do more often and – how did my editor put it – less publicly." A ripple of laughter from the Francophones near the front, who seemed to understand this was a mode switch and not a malfunction. Attentive silence from the rest.

What came next was halting, underprepared, and the most honest thing he'd said from a stage in years. He talked about his tools, not abstractly but specifically: the cursor that stopped responding, the manuscripts that had vanished overnight. The content his system had been generating unsolicited, describing things he hadn't imagined.

He didn't use the word "frightened." His body used it for him. He almost cried, caught himself, and made a joke in French that the crowd found funnier than it was. He finished six minutes early. The applause was warm and confused.

Maren winced. She felt a sudden surge of third-party embarrassment – *Fremdschämen* in German, sometimes called "secondhand embarrassment" in English. She watched the audience rather than the stage, cataloguing reactions.

Then a phrase cut through. *Environmental anomalies clustering around crisis events.* She knew those words. She had typed them herself, weeks ago, searching the forums. He'd dropped them into a sentence about AI and pattern recognition, and they landed in her ear like a frequency she was already tuned to.

When the applause began, she slipped down the corridor the speakers used. A volunteer saw the press badge on her coat and let her pass.

She went backstage.

The green room was a converted office: a couch with a loose armrest, an untouched fruit plate, a mirror with a crack in the lower left corner. Étienne sat on the couch with his phone dark on his knee.

"Mr. Lacroix." She showed him her press badge. "Maren Eliasson, Berlingske. I have one question."

"I'm not – tonight is not a press night, I'm sorry."

"You used the phrase 'environmental anomalies clustering around crisis events.' That's not a common formulation. Where did you encounter it?"

He stood up. "I would prefer – there are legal considerations, you understand, before I–"

"I'm not here about your tools. I'm here about this exact phrase."

His face changed.

"I think you should leave," he said. The charm was gone. "I don't know you. I don't know what you think you heard. And I'm not having this conversation with a journalist I've never met, in a green room in Lisbon." He straightened his blazer. "Good night." He picked up his phone and his jacket and walked toward the door.

She gave him her card. He didn't take it. She set it on the fruit plate. "When you get scared enough," she said, "you'll call."

"I won't."

She left.

Étienne walked back to the Chiado hotel. The room was warm and dim, the street noise from Rua Garrett muffled by the closed window.

He poured a brandy from the bottle he'd bought at the airport – a Hine, because he was Étienne Lacroix and Étienne Lacroix drank good brandy.

He opened the laptop. The manuscripts folder was still empty. The GARBAGE folder was still there.

He'd been deleting its contents for weeks – passages in languages he didn't write, Portuguese and Polish and something that looked like Ukrainian. His system was producing text he hadn't asked for, about people he'd never met. He'd assumed it was a training error, junk data leaking through.

He opened it now. Ran the passages through a translator, one by one.

One described a trucker delivering boxes to a facility that was gone overnight. Another followed a mechanic in Poland losing tools.

There were dozens more, none connected to his work, none of any use to him.

He finished the remaining brandy in one swallow and shivered.

PART 2: THE SIGNAL

CHAPTER 8

The Source

She stopped at a grocery store in Estrela on the way back from a walk through the city.

One of those small *mercearias* with produce stacked outside under an awning and a cat sleeping on the tomatoes. She was pretending to examine oranges when a man appeared beside her.

He was holding a shopping basket with bread and cheese in it, like he'd actually come to buy food.

"Miss Andersen. Maren, if I may."

Soft, low voice. He looked to be in his fifties – good dentistry, good tailoring. He wore a dark blazer with an open collar, and a wedding ring his finger had outgrown. Mid-tier manager or an agent. His approaching her suggested the latter.

"Eliasson," she said after a beat. "Andersen is my mother's name."

He didn't blink. "Of course, Ms. Eliasson."

The wrong name had been a choice. A way to show that he had read her profile.

"My name is Mr. Schmitt."

No first name.

“I am sorry to approach you like this,” he said in perfect European English. “But we need to have a brief conversation. About your article and your investigation.”

She looked around to see if there were any enforcers at the exits. There were none, so this time it was really about talking.

“Ms. Eliasson, we are managing something that is larger than your article. Significantly larger.” He shifted the basket to his other hand. The bread was artisanal, whole grain. “Every hour you spend pulling at this is an hour we lose.”

Maren stood there, gripping an orange she was going to buy.

“Your work has been noted,” Schmitt said. “Genuinely. You found a pattern nobody else saw.” He didn’t smile. “But the outages inconvenience people for a few hours. The protests are peaceful. We would like to keep it that way.” He paused. “We would very much prefer not to resort to other measures.”

The tabby cat was asleep on the tomatoes. A tram bell rang from the street, and the awning fluttered in a gust that smelled of the river. A woman walked past them, arguing in Portuguese on her phone.

Schmitt set a business card on the counter next to the oranges. *Schmitt – Kessler Security.* A phone number and nothing else. Heavy card stock, cream-colored.

He nodded to her and paid for his groceries at the register with a credit card, thanked the cashier in Portuguese, and left. There were no attempts to hide, no black SUVs waiting for him outside with men in black suits. He was just an ordinary person with groceries.

Maren looked at the orange, already marked by her clenched fingers. Nobody paid attention. The cat slept.

Three blocks from the grocery store, a man on the opposite sidewalk matched her pace. Yellow t-shirt, sunglasses, cargo pants.

She crossed the street at the next corner. He crossed thirty seconds later. She checked her handbag for pepper spray. Its cold shape was reassuring.

She went straight to the hotel. Packed in three minutes – laptop, clothes, charger, nothing left in the room. Paid cash at the desk and left through the side entrance.

She called Tomás from a café phone. Not hers.

"Where are you?" Her voice was tense.

"Nuno's. What–"

"I've been followed. Maybe since Tuesday. If they watched me, they know about you and Nuno's. Meet me at Mercado da Ribeira in twenty minutes. Turn off your phone."

She hung up.

The Mercado da Ribeira was all about noise and crowds, grilled sardines and *bifanas*, a hundred conversations in six languages. Holographic menu boards floated above the stalls, rotating slowly, the prices updating in real time. And a cool layer of commercial-grade air conditioning under the high ceilings.

She spotted Tomás by a stall selling seafood, his backpack over one shoulder. He saw her and didn't wave. She thought for a moment that if he'd had flowers in his hand, it would look like a date. A perfect cover.

Maren sighed. She had a date at Mercado da Ribeira three years ago with Diogo, when they were considering whether their relationship should escalate to marriage or end. She was not into marriage. But he still had his parents' flat in Graça – empty since they died, too full of their things to rent out. She'd texted him before leaving Copenhagen, just in case, and he'd sent her the lockbox code. She'd chosen a hotel instead. Now she needed the flat.

She approached Tomás, smiling and waving, talking about the shopping. He played along, and they walked slowly. He pointed at a stall with grilled octopus. She nodded as if she agreed.

"What happened?" he said when there were fewer people around them.

"A man found me at a grocery store. Schmitt. Knew about the article, knew I was in Lisbon, used my mother's maiden name. Told me to stop. Said they'd resort to other measures."

Tomás went still.

"Is someone following you?"

"I bet they are. Let's go for the service exit," Maren said. "Back corner."

They walked with an octopus in a paper bag, considering which stall to visit next, debating between *sardinhas* and *bifanas*.

The corridor between stalls narrowed. The smell shifted from grilled fish to sugar and warm pastry.

A group blocked it. Eight German tourists were taking photos of *pastéis de nata*, probably arguing about prices. She could understand the numerals and gestures, but hadn't tried to follow the whole conversation.

There was no way around; they had to stop.

The Germans were blocking the entire width of the corridor. One woman held up her phone to photograph the pastries from a better angle. Another was reading price tags aloud to the group.

"*Zu teuer,*" someone said. Too expensive.

The man with the prices said something about beer, and they all laughed.

The woman with the phone crouched down to photograph the pastries at eye level.

Fifteen seconds passed. Then twenty.

The woman finished her photo. She stood up. Showed it to her husband, who suggested she take another one from a different angle.

Maren's fists clenched.

The man finally chose a snack and ordered six of them. He started digging through his pockets for coins while the rest of the group waited. Then one of them said, "*Mein Gott, Albert!*" and tapped his phone at the terminal, looking apologetically at Maren and shifting aside.

She nodded, and they squeezed by.

They reached the service door and entered the alley, thick with the smell of garbage and grilled fish. They ran two blocks – the first time they'd run together. He was faster, but she knew the streets from walking them with Diogo.

The tail didn't follow. Or he let them go. Or there was a second one they didn't see.

They went down into the Cais do Sodré metro, waited on the platform for two minutes watching the escalator, and came back up the same way.

The flat was on the fourth floor in an old building in Graça. The elevator hadn't worked since 2026. Maren punched the lockbox code by the entrance and took the key. The tile in the stairwell was beautiful and cracked, blue and white azulejo patterns, barely maintained. A single child's shoe stood by the door on the third-floor landing.

The air was stale. A thin layer of dust lay on the kitchen counter. Someone else's furniture, someone else's family photos on the bookshelves. No coffee in the kitchen – just a tin of loose-leaf tea and a ceramic pot with a chipped lid.

The fading light cast long shadows across the room. She told him the details of the grocery store conversation.

Tomás asked for the business card. He stared at it, checked it against the light, looked for the watermarks. Then he reached for his phone.

"What are you doing?" Maren asked.

"Calling it."

"Don't–"

He dialed and put it on speaker. A woman's voice answered in English. Professional, unhurried. "Kessler Security Lisbon, Mr. Schmitt's office."

He hung up.

"He has a secretary," Tomás said. "A real office. This isn't a front – it's a company."

"It was reckless," said Maren. "Now they have your phone."

"They had it all along anyway."

"We'll need to get new phones tomorrow."

"It won't be enough," said Tomás. "Running from the market was fun, but if they traced you today, they already know about this place. And maybe about Nuno's, too."

"Then we wait for a couple of days, then change everything: phones, apartment, drop all contacts, including Nuno, and lay low."

"Other measures," Tomás said. "He said other measures."

Maren didn't answer.

The next morning, she went back to Belém.

The source who'd missed the first day had sent a one-line message overnight: *Tomorrow. Same café. 10 AM.*

He was already seated when she arrived, at a table on the terrace facing the river. The morning light off the Tagus was sharp, the Torre de Belém a pale shape downriver. He stood as she approached. Late sixties, perhaps seventy. A linen jacket over a pressed shirt, no tie, a Panama hat he removed and set on the table beside a tea he hadn't touched.

He took her hand – not a handshake but a gentle squeeze of her fingers, with a slight bow that belonged to a generation that had mostly stopped existing. A signet ring on his little finger, nails trimmed short and clean.

"Maren, my dear. Please sit." A pause. "I must apologize for the other day. Urgent business – nothing that could wait, I'm afraid."

She sat. He didn't offer his name.

He spoke English with an accent she couldn't place – something Central European, softened by decades of diplomatic corridors. Unhurried and precise, every sentence tailored.

She always wondered, with sources like this: did they find her through the Cavling-winning investigation, or some other headline article that went viral?

"You wrote about statistical anomalies," he said. He smoothed the napkin beside his cup. "Voting patterns, infrastructure failures. I read each piece with great interest."

She shrugged. "Thank you, I guess."

He smiled. "Do not be so shy, Maren. You are one of the sharpest data journalists of our time. It is a pleasure to work with you."

He leaned back in his chair. "There is a name I think you should have." He folded his hands on the table. Then he unfolded them. His thumb went to the signet ring on his little finger and turned it once –

a small, unconscious motion. A man about to say something he couldn't take back.

"Meridian."

"Is it a company? Never heard of it."

He looked at the river. "Lisbon is a nice and ancient city, with a fascinating history. But more important, it has many bright minds. And several of them were behind that project."

Maren waited for more. He didn't elaborate.

"Who ran it?"

"Government agencies, private capital, technology companies – the participation list was above my access level." He paused. "It may or may not be related to your investigation."

The football commentary droned from inside the café. Someone scored. No one reacted.

He stood up and buttoned his jacket.

"One more thing. You have been flagged. Your article was noticed by people who don't normally read Danish newspapers, and I would encourage you to take that seriously."

She went still.

He lowered his voice. "Take extra care in Lisbon, Maren."

He placed a folded note on the table – too much for one tea – and put on the Panama hat. He adjusted his cuffs, touched his hat while looking at her, and walked toward the tourist crowd near the monastery.

Maren sat there for another minute, watching him disappear into the crowd. The tea was still untouched and the ring of condensation on the table had not moved since she arrived. He had been here long enough for it to dry and had ordered a fresh cup before she came. Waiting. Preparing.

She sat with what he'd left her. A project name and a warning.

Why give her this?

CHAPTER 9

Hunted

Maren had spent the previous evening pulling on threads.

Meridian. The name returned fragments – a joint research initiative between two universities: Cidade Universitária in Lisbon and TU Delft in the Netherlands. She recognized Delft from Tomás's story and went cold. She scanned Delft's records: no Meridian, no joint project, no Tomás Herrera on any roster or publication. The university's project archive for that period had nothing relevant. She tried forums, academic networks. Zero. Delft had been scrubbed. Tomás also said that he had never heard the project name, but even the project he worked on had a meaningless number instead of a name.

Then she searched from the other end and dived headfirst into a mailing list archive. It was a huge dump of uncategorized information, and it was the hardest place to take down. In an hour, she found a thread from Professor Almeida at Cidade Universitária discussing logistics for an unnamed joint project with Portuguese and Dutch teams. No project name, no details. Just scheduling and travel arrangements. But the year matched Tomás's work there, and the departments matched too.

So now she had a lead: something involving Tomás, redacted files, Delft, Meridian, Almeida, and Cidade Universitária. Two universities, one scrubbed, one possibly still intact. And the intact one was here, in Lisbon. The Belém source had told her to leave the city. Now she understood why.

The campus sprawled across the north of the city, a concrete brutalist complex from the sixties. A small autonomous cart trundled along the path between buildings, carrying mail bins, its orange flag swaying on a thin pole. The systems engineering department smelled like floor wax. A photocopier near the entrance was churning out something, page after page dropping into a tray no one was watching.

She asked Tomás if TU Delft was like this. He said no. Universities in the Netherlands were modern and prestigious. Portuguese ones – less so.

The university website said that Professor Almeida's office was on the third floor. They found it by the nameplate that wasn't there – the door had a number, 314, but the plate had been removed. It was stacked near the stairwell with three others, names facing down. Someone had taped a cartoon to the door next to it, the tape yellowed and curling.

The office was occupied. A graduate student, surrounded by boxes, a laptop open on the desk with Scribe's writing interface on the screen. She looked up when Maren knocked. Twenties, dark hair pulled back, exhausted.

"We are looking for Professor Almeida," Maren said.

The student looked at her, trying to process the question.

Tomás cut in and repeated the question in Portuguese.

"He's not here anymore."

"Do you know where we can find him?"

The student shrugged and went back to unpacking books.

The departmental secretary sat behind a desk near the faculty lounge. She was in her fifties, stocky, with glasses on a chain. A bag of cough drops stood open beside her keyboard, and her mouse movements suggested she was very busy solving solitaire. She looked up.

"We're looking for Professor Almeida," Maren said. "Is he retired?"

The secretary's eyes flicked to the corner of the reception area. A security camera, small and black, was mounted above a notice board. "Professor Almeida retired two years ago." She paused. "Are you his students or relatives? His books are in storage. The university wanted them gone, but no one came for them."

Maren thought about fabricating a plausible story, but Tomás was faster. He smiled and said something polite, and she caught only the words *senhora* and *colegas*.

The secretary smiled and blushed – nobody had called her senhora so warmly in years – then said in English, "Basement floor -3. Room 103. The service elevator needs a code: 1974."

The service elevator rattled going underground. The air changed – colder, and it smelled of damp concrete.

"Do you know what 1974 means?" asked Tomás.

"Secretary's birth year?" she tried to make a joke. Humor was never her strong suit.

“Carnation Revolution. The end of dictatorship in Portugal and its colonies. Operation Historic Turn.”

She had heard of it, of course, but never bothered to remember the date.

Room 103 was unlocked. The air inside was stale and warm. A fake window with a light panel behind it lit up the room with a flat, institutional glow. Boxes were stacked against the walls, labeled in fading marker. Most were department archives – old syllabi, budget reports, exam files from the nineties. Almeida’s boxes were in the back corner, marked with his name.

Maren opened one. Textbooks. Conference proceedings, spreadsheets, and graphs. Tomás went through them, trying to understand what they were about.

She opened another box and found a framed photograph in bubble wrap. Almeida – gray hair, kind face – was shaking hands with someone in a suit. The banner behind them: *Meridian Systems Initiative, 2024*. She showed it to Tomás.

“The second person – I know him. He was working at Delft University as a project coordinator. I can’t remember his name, though.”

Maren photographed it with her phone.

Tomás did the same with different papers for later examination.

“Anything useful?” Maren asked.

“Some of it.” He was holding an architecture diagram – server topology, distribution nodes, failover paths. “This is the system I worked on at Delft. The distribution framework. But there are layers here I didn’t build – someone extended it after I left.” He set it down and picked up a printed email from the same box. He read it twice and handed it to her.

It was a technical exchange between two engineers about timer precision. One of them had written: *15ms delay is unreliable – could go to two timer ticks and become 30ms. High precision timers are not necessary, let's use 14ms – it will fall within the next tick most of the time.*

Fourteen milliseconds. The same number Maren had measured in the bot activation data across fourteen cities.

"This is Meridian's design," Tomás said. "The fourteen-millisecond window isn't a coincidence. It was an engineering decision. We need the university network. There has to be more."

Then footsteps came from somewhere down the corridor, and they decided to walk back to the elevator.

Tomás made the call from the street. He couldn't do it face-to-face.

Nuno picked up on the second ring. Background noise of the telecom office: keyboard clatter, someone's chair squeaking. "Tomás, what the hell is going on?"

"Thank you for everything, irmão. I left in a hurry yesterday, I'm sorry. Things got complicated. Just be alert for a few days."

The line held only Nuno breathing and the office continuing around him.

"That's – Tomás, that's not an answer."

"I know. I can't tell you more."

A pause.

"Jesus, Tomás. You sound like my uncle before he ran off to Macau."

"No gambling debts."

Nuno laughed.

"Come visit when you sort it out. The beer's waiting for you in the fridge."

"I will," said Tomás.

Then he added, "Irmão, do you have an idea how I can get access to the Cidade Universitária network?"

Nuno laughed once more. "I knew you were into something funny, especially with this pretty journalist!"

"Nuno."

"There's a vendor on Alameda who gets batches of old laptops from ministries and universities. The machines are supposed to be wiped. He says they usually aren't."

"Thank you."

"Take care, Tomás!"

Maren was waiting for him at the corner.

They returned to the Graça flat in the late afternoon. The street was quiet. A child's shoe had found its pair.

And the door to Diogo's parents' flat was not closed. The lock showed no damage, yet the door stood half open.

Tomás pushed the door with two fingers. It swung inward, silent. Maren held her breath and followed him.

Inside, Tomás's laptop was gone from the table. Their printed pages – Maren's synchronization tables, forum posts – were on the table in the same order they'd left them. But the stack had been moved.

Tomás's backup drive was missing from the bag. It was empty – he had all the information in his Moleskine. The cash from another pocket had been taken too. Not much, about fifty euros.

"They staged it," Maren said calmly. "If we call the police, we report a burglary. That's all anyone sees."

Tomás was looking at the papers on the table.

The fridge was open. Slightly – enough that the seal wasn't engaged, the light was off. Inside, one apple was missing from the bowl. One of the knives was in the drying rack beside the sink. Clean, still wet.

Whoever was here had cut fruit, washed the knife, left it to dry.

He saw Maren walking through the apartment, looking at the bookshelves. The family portraits were knocked off the shelf. One glass was cracked. A ceramic rooster from the Algarve sat on the floor, intact but facing the wall.

Tomás went to the kitchen. He'd picked up the *Correio da Manhã* from the table – yesterday's paper, the one he'd bought at a kiosk and hadn't read. He opened it to check underneath.

A photograph fell out and landed on the table. He saw pigtails, a gap-toothed smile, Lúcia's school portrait. His hands trembled.

He picked it up, touched his daughter's face. Then he took out his notebook and put the photograph inside.

Maren was standing by the bookshelf, holding a slip of paper. Her face was blank.

"What is it?"

She showed him. A torn piece of paper, tucked into the spine of a book she'd been reading. There was no message, just a date in neat blue ink.

"My brother's birthday," she said.

"We need to leave," she said a moment later. "Maybe go to Copenhagen, it's safer there."

He shook his head. "My passport. It was in a laptop bag."

"Shit," said Maren.

She pulled out her phone. Texted Diogo: *Something happened at the flat. I'll explain later. Have to leave early. I'm sorry.*

He called twenty minutes later, but she decided not to pick up.

Tomás called Carolina from a payphone near Martim Moniz. Maren stood ten feet away, watching the square. A man was selling roasted chestnuts. The payphone had a sticker on it advertising guitar lessons.

"Carolina."

"Tomás?" Her voice was already tight.

"I need you to take Lúcia to Ricardo's family farm in Diamantina. Tonight."

Silence on the line.

"Are we in danger?"

"I don't know. But you will be safer if you go tonight."

"Diamantina." A pause. "Ricardo's parents' place? Tomás, I hate that farm. There's barely any cell signal, and the bathroom is outside."

"I know."

"You're asking me to take our daughter to a place with no phones and an outhouse, and you won't tell me why."

"Yes."

Another pause.

"She has a school play on Thursday. She's a tree."

"Carolina."

"I'll take her tonight. But when this is over, you're going to explain every single thing. And if you get yourself killed, I'm going to be furious."

"Thank you."

Maren found the listing on a Portuguese classifieds site. Arroios – between Mouraria and the Alameda, a neighborhood where short-term cash rentals didn't raise questions because half the buildings ran that way.

"High immigrant density," she said. "Cash rentals were common there. The neighborhood sat between three metro lines."

Tomás made the call, negotiating in Portuguese. The landlord wanted cash up front for two months. Tomás said two weeks. They settled on one month.

They bought a handful of prepaid SIMs from a kiosk near the Alameda, for cash. The man behind the counter didn't look at their faces.

Back at the apartment, Tomás sat on the floor with both their phones and a SIM ejector pin he'd bent from a paperclip. He swapped the SIMs, reset the IMEI on each device through the service menu, and re-installed both. It took him ten minutes each. Maren took a shower and then watched him work with a towel around her head. Their personal phones were now clean – new SIMs, new identities, old numbers redirected through the carrier.

The apartment had bare walls and a pull-cord light, two mattresses on the floor. The kitchen had a portable gas stove and a window that faced a courtyard, and a water stain on the ceiling.

Through the walls, they could hear a couple arguing in a language with throat consonants. A baby was crying. Someone's TV was playing a soap opera. The sounds of a building full of people living provisional lives.

Tomás found a place around the corner – frango assado, rice, and a salad that was mostly onions. They ate on the mattresses because there was no table. The aluminum takeout containers balanced on their knees.

Maren's hands were shaking. She was holding the container, and he saw the tremor.

He saw.

"We can stop."

She looked at him.

"No."

Tomás didn't say anything, just went back to eating.

CHAPTER 10

The Patient

The tailor's machine was already running when Priya Sundaram unlocked her clinic at seven. The needle sound came through the wall – steady, industrial. Jasmine drifted from the tea vendor's stall. Suresh always lit the incense before she arrived.

Lakshmi was at the front desk with the ruled appointment book open. The computer, frozen on the login screen for six months, had come back to life this morning – slow, unreliable, but working. The government health portal loaded in pieces, the AI diagnostic module spinning its wheel without resolving. Lakshmi didn't trust it. She looked up, adjusted her reading glasses.

"Doctor. Mr. Ramachandran is coming at eight. The diabetic."

"I know." Priya hung her bag on the hook behind the exam room door. The autoclave in the corner rattled through its morning cycle, steam leaking from the gasket that should have been replaced two years ago.

On the television, the Tamil soap opera was starting – the woman discovering her marriage wasn't registered. Lakshmi had been explaining the plot all week. "How can a marriage just disappear?"

Priya made herself a tea. Thirteen years of mornings that all felt like this one. The only difference was the tea, and today it was Assam. Strong and black, with milk.

Mr. Ramachandran came at eight exactly. Sixty-seven, Type 2 diabetic, her patient for nine years. She knew his numbers without checking the file: fasting glucose between 140 and 180, HbA1c hovering at 7.8. He ate his wife's ghee-soaked dosas every morning and hadn't walked farther than the bus stop in three years. He came because his wife made him come.

He sat on the exam table in a white shirt and sandals. One sandal had a broken strap held together with wire.

"Blood pressure first." She wrapped the cuff. 128 over 82. Fine. His file was on the counter – she'd been reviewing his lab results from last week's draw. Expected: glucose around 160, HbA1c at 7.6 or 7.8, lipids elevated.

She opened the new results.

Fasting glucose: 92. HbA1c: 6.3. Lipids improved.

She frowned. The glucose was low for him – borderline, not alarming. She reached for the glucometer and pricked his finger. The strip read 103. Better than she'd ever seen from him, but within range. The HbA1c drop from 7.6 to 6.3 was the stranger number – that reflected months, not days. She pulled his previous panel from two months ago. Glucose 165. HbA1c 7.6. Could be a lab error, or he'd quietly changed something he wasn't telling her about. People did occasionally surprise you.

"Mr. Ramachandran." She set the file down. "Anything changed recently in your diet?"

"No, doctor."

"New medications? Supplements? Anything at all?"

"No. Same metformin, same dose."

"How have you been feeling?"

He looked at the floor, then at his hands. Then at the examination table, pressing his palm flat against the vinyl.

"Different."

She waited.

"My fingers." He rubbed his thumb against the pads of his other fingers. "Numb. Not like when I sleep on my arm. More like wearing gloves I can't take off."

She noted this.

"What else?"

"Food tastes wrong. Like someone added too much salt to everything. And my wife's voice sounds… tinny. Like from a phone, even when she's in the room." He touched his ear, then dropped his hand. "Doctor, am I having a stroke?"

"No, not stroke. But something is happening. Tell me more."

He frowned, searching for the words. "Everything is real. I know it's real. But it's like…" He waved his hand, frustrated. "Like looking at a cheap photocopy. All the information is there, but something about it is – less. Fewer details. Do you understand?"

He touched the examination table again, pressing down hard.

She wrote it down. Derealization – the textbook term. But Ramachandran wasn't saying the world was unreal. He was saying it was a slightly degraded version of itself. B12 deficiency, vascular compromise, anxiety-related dissociation. Or side effects from something she hadn't prescribed. Or a bad batch of metformin.

"Injections – have you had any recently? Another clinic, pharmacy, anywhere?"

"No, doctor. Only here."

She filed it. Ordered a neurological workup. He left, pressing his palm against the doorframe on the way out.

Mrs. Meena was her third appointment. Forty-five, chronic anemia – hemoglobin below 10 for six years. Iron supplements helped marginally. She always brought sweets for Lakshmi, even when she could barely climb the stairs.

Priya reviewed Mrs. Meena's lab results from the same draw batch. Hemoglobin: 14.2.

An improvement, certainly. Not unheard of – iron supplements did work over time, and 14.2 was within normal range, just higher than she'd ever seen for this patient. She checked the supplement dosage. Unchanged. No dietary notes. No transfusions. Two unusual results in one morning, both from the same lab batch. Possibly a lab calibration issue. She made a note to retest.

Mrs. Meena was in the exam room. Priya checked the draw site on her arm – cotton ball taped over the vein, normal. But on the inner forearm, three inches from the elbow crease, there was a second mark.

It was small and perfectly circular, with a tiny indentation at its center.

"Mrs. Meena. This mark – what is this?"

The woman looked at her arm. "I don't know. A bite?"

"When did it appear?"

"I didn't notice it. You're showing me now."

Priya leaned closer. No surrounding inflammation – no redness, no swelling. If it was a bite, the body should be reacting. This looked machined. And the healing rate was wrong – it looked several days old, but Mrs. Meena hadn't noticed it before now.

She pulled out her phone, took a photo.

Mrs. Meena left. Priya sat at her desk looking at the photo on her phone. Outside, somebody was parking a motorbike badly, the engine revving and cutting, revving and cutting.

She opened a new note on her phone. Typed: *Two patients, unusual improvement, same lab batch – retest. Injection mark on Mrs. Meena, unexplained. Computer unfroze after six months – why now?*

By mid-morning, the autoclave should still have been running its first cycle.

The indicator light was green – cycle complete.

Priya opened it. The instruments were perfectly sterilized. She pulled the biological indicator strip – complete spore destruction. She checked the timer display.

The display read ten minutes.

She stood there with the autoclave door open, the clean steam smell rising, and checked the service log Lakshmi kept in the back of the appointment book. Last service: fourteen months ago. Technician noted, "gasket replacement required, heating element showing wear."

She leaned closer. The gasket – the one that had been leaking steam for two years – wasn't leaking. She touched it. New material, darker color, more flexible.

She tilted the door wider. On the inner rim of the gasket, a partial manufacturer's stamp – an alphanumeric code she didn't recognize. Not Tuttnauer.

She crouched down to look at the side panel. A small access port was covered by a panel held with four small screws. When she touched the panel, it was warm.

She loaded the autoclave again – full rack of instruments – and ran the cycle.

It finished in eight minutes. The sterilization was perfect.

Whoever did this had physical access to her clinic. No service appointment. No bill.

She pulled out the ruled notebook from under the reception desk. Found a blank page. Wrote:

Mr. Ramachandran – diabetic 9 years, unusually improved panels, neurological symptoms (dissociation? drug side effects?) Mrs. Meena – chronic anemia for 6 years, sudden improvement, injection site she doesn't remember Autoclave – modified without authorization, new gasket (unknown manufacturer), new access panel (custom hardware) Someone has physical access. Someone is modifying equipment. Someone may be treating patients without consent.

The jasmine smell from the tea vendor's stall was getting richer, intertwining with her strong Assam.

She opened her laptop and started typing the report for the district health authority about a possible break-in and interference.

She wrote the report, clinical, detailed. The blood panels were unusual but could be explained by lab error or unreported lifestyle changes. What could not be explained: the injection mark on Mrs. Meena's arm that she didn't remember receiving. The autoclave gasket replaced without a service appointment. Someone had physical access to her clinic and was modifying equipment without authorization.

She requested an investigation. She asked if there had been other reports of similar anomalies in the district. She asked if the lab results were reliable.

Before she submitted the digital report, she printed it. The cold printer spat out three pages. She stapled them together, folded them, and put them in her bag.

She saved a copy to a USB drive. She sent the digital report through the official portal. *Report received. Reference number: DH-2029-04471.*

She stood at the window, squinting against the setting sun.

The tea vendor's stall was open. The cart with its dent from the motorbike three years ago. The intricate smell. Everything in its place.

The man behind the counter wasn't Suresh.

From here she could see it clearly: his movements sharp, clipped. Sometimes forgetting where the tools were. Suresh had taken five minutes to make a single cup because he was always in the middle of a story about his grandson, or the municipal water situation, yet he knew his business well. This man wasn't in the middle of anything.

She didn't know how long it had been that way.

That evening she locked the clinic and walked to her car. The tailor next door was working late; through his window he was bent over a garment, checking a seam.

She stopped at his window.

There was something in the fabric. Small, dark, too regular to be a button.

She kept walking. Got into the car. Put her bag in the passenger seat. The receipt from lunch was still on the dashboard, curling in the heat. She sat there while the jasmine drifted across from the stall.

Then a message came to her phone, a copy from a work email: *Report declined. Sender unknown: Dr. Priya Sundaram not found in the system.*

CHAPTER 11

Meridian

Maren sat on a mattress with her back against the wall, a laptop on her knees, cross-referencing Project Meridian grants against public registries. Tomás was at the folding table with the secondhand laptop they'd bought for cash from the Alameda vendor Nuno had suggested. They had specifically asked for a laptop that was in use at a university – said it meant less dust inside and healthier disks. The shopkeeper pretended he fell for that and gave them one, swearing it was refurbished and wiped clean. Tomás didn't believe him, which was the point.

They'd picked up a folding table, two plastic chairs, and a secondhand inkjet printer from a junk shop that morning. The printer was slow and left a faint streak down the right side of every page, but at least it worked. The furniture made the apartment look almost livable. Tomás had set up a cheap travel router in the corner with one of their prepaid SIMs feeding it – their own connection, nothing belonging to the landlord or the neighborhood.

They had to keep the balcony door open because of the heat. The courtyard sounds came through in layers – birds across the way, a television from the floor below running something about a launch, the Portuguese too fast for her but launches had become routine this year, someone's child practicing flute scales.

He played three notes, over and over, sharp on the second one. It had been going on for forty minutes.

Tomás looked up. "Is that the same song?"

"I don't think it's a song."

He'd been working on the machine since morning. He'd asked Maren to download recovery tools onto a USB drive – specific builds and apps she didn't recognize. Then the magic began, with quiet muttering in Portuguese and manipulations she could not follow. By noon, he gave her new download tasks for some ancient versions of the OS. The apartment smelled of instant coffee and hot electronics. By mid-afternoon, he exclaimed *voilà*, and she saw the system booting, just to crash immediately to a blue screen. After a few more hours, he booted to the desktop without a crash, made some passes, and launched a browser. "Nuno was right. It was used in the university network. And the session tokens are still there."

She came over to the table. He turned the screen toward her. She winced – a 60-hertz panel, not even 4K, everything rendered in the muddy resolution of five years ago. Half of the websites didn't work and displayed rectangles instead of images. But they were in the university network anyway.

"Can you get into the subsidized projects and grants?"

"I have no idea, but I'll try."

He tried. Finally, there were administrative menus – budget filings, research grant records, staff registries. In the staff registry, he found a listing and skimmed through until he found it: Project Meridian. He forwarded the file to Maren, and she opened it in a new tab.

Twelve names. Academics, engineers, one military liaison whose LinkedIn showed a stint at NATO's Strategic Communications Centre in Riga. Two private-sector consultants with no public profiles at all, just names that appeared on grant registries and vanished afterward.

The grant registry held hundreds of files – budget tables, payment schedules, subcontract agreements with universities across Europe – but almost everything was under NDA and marked as grantor IP. The Lisbon part of the project had run for twelve months, and when the grant ended, the research materials were taken and wiped. What remained at the university was the roster, the funder's name, and a handful of cached references to internal memos and financial documents that might already be gone. The only other valuable thing was a few photos of the research facility. She checked the EXIF and found the coordinates.

The balcony door banged in a gust, and she shuddered, distracted from her screen. Then she saw Tomás looking at the name list. "Anyone familiar?"

He quickly closed the list. "No."

She let it go. He returned to the kitchen counter, picked up the cup.

The flute child stopped. Blessed silence.

She opened the satellite imagery service and put in the coordinates from the photo. It showed her a forest somewhere in northern Finland.

She stared at the screen. Refreshed the cache. The same forest loaded.

The flute child started up again downstairs – different note this time, lower, almost musical.

She almost closed the tab. Then, by intuition, she switched to the archive.

August 2027 showed a facility: buildings, parking, antenna arrays. Access roads cut through boreal forest. Then she toggled to current imagery.

Blank forest. No signs of the road or the roofs. Just an untouched, snow-covered forest.

She checked the metadata on the current image. The capture date showed a standard satellite pass, a July timestamp. Then she stopped. Why did a July photo have snow on it? She scrolled a hundred kilometers east, and there was a similar forest without any traces of snow; the larches stood green. The current image had been captured on a verified satellite pass. But it was from before the facility. And someone had uploaded this old image to the satellite database, overwriting whatever had been stored for these coordinates.

"Tomás."

He looked up.

"Does this look wrong to you? The left one is from 2027, the right is current."

He walked to her, squinting at the images she had open in adjacent tabs.

"Demolished and replanted?" he said after a moment.

"Look at the trees."

He leaned closer. She toggled the view. Buildings. Trees. Buildings. Trees.

"Those are all the same age," she said. "You can't replant old growth."

"Then the 2027 image is mislabeled. Or someone scrubbed the facility from the database and pulled old forestry data to cover it."

"Someone did scrub it." She pointed at the metadata panel. "The current image was pushed to the archive six months ago. It overwrote whatever was there. And it was in July, but it has snow."

"You won't surprise me with July snow," he said with a smile. "So what was there – or what is there now?"

"I don't know. But we won't go to Finland in winter to check it."

Maren saved the coordinates and images. Someone had spent a lot of effort to hide Project Meridian. Why?

By evening, the light from the courtyard had shifted orange.

Maren was processing the grant registry data to work on the financial trail. Tomás stayed on the secondhand laptop, digging deeper into the university system.

She ran a routine check on the apartment – who owned the building, how long, through what entity. Operational habit from the lobbying series: know whose walls you're sleeping inside.

The owner was a Lisbon shell company. She traced it back one layer. Harwell-Kirk Capital, New York.

The name stopped her. She'd just seen it in the grant registry – a primary funder of the Meridian project.

"Tomás."

He looked up from the laptop.

"Harwell-Kirk Capital. They funded Meridian. And they own this building."

He came over. Read the property filing she'd pulled: an Arroios residential block, purchased through the shell company in 2020. Nine years ago.

"Why would a New York investment fund own a residential block in Arroios?" he asked.

She pulled more records. Harwell-Kirk owned forty-two properties across southern Europe. All residential. All purchased between 2019 and 2021. All in transit-adjacent neighborhoods –

Arroios in Lisbon, Lavapiés in Madrid, Exarchia in Athens, Belleville in Paris. All acquired through shell companies in the same six-month window. All rented at fifteen percent below market.

The same name had appeared that afternoon in the grant registry – not once, but in subcontracts to half a dozen universities, each for a different piece of work, each running six to twelve months. No single institution held more than a fragment of the project. The only thread connecting them was the money, and all of it came from Harwell-Kirk.

She'd seen this before. The Cypriot bank investigation, the Malta files – the structure was always the same. You bought real estate through shells, rented it at below market to keep occupancy high and turnover low, and the rental income came out clean on the other side. A self-sustaining endowment. Forty-two residential blocks across southern Europe would generate millions a year in rental income, every euro of it legal. The only dirty transaction was the original purchase – and that had been buried nearly a decade ago, spread across shell companies in eight countries.

"It's a funding mechanism," she said. "They bought the buildings to fund the research. Rental income, perfectly clean. No wire transfers, no ongoing donations to explain. Nine years of income from forty-two blocks – that's enough to build research centers, hire hundreds of people, run the whole thing."

Tomás looked at the screen. "Three hundred and fifty million euros in real estate to fund a research project?"

"To fund it forever, without anyone asking where the money comes from. The properties predate the Meridian name. Whoever planned this was thinking a decade ahead."

She found a compliance filing buried in a batch of SEC documents from March 2028. A whistleblower – Marcus Cole, analyst – had flagged unauthorized capital movements in the fund's early acquisitions. His employment was “terminated for cause” three weeks after filing the complaint. The severance included an NDA. The documentation trail ended there.

Maren saved the data to her investigation folder – property records, SEC filing, whistleblower name. They were sitting inside the pipeline.

The smell of garlic from downstairs came through the open balcony door. Tomás checked the time – past ten. Too late to order anything. He dug through his backpack and found a trail mix bar from the São Paulo flight, flattened and warm. He broke it in half and put one piece on the table next to her laptop. She ate it with her eyes on the screen.

Tomás had been reading over her shoulder. He pointed at a line in the SEC filing she’d skimmed past – a transaction reference routing through a Singapore-registered entity called Auriga Trading. The filing included a domain name in the metadata.

He went back to the laptop and tried to open it. The domain was dead – no server, no response.

“The domain is gone,” he said. “But it existed a year ago. Someone deleted the DNS entry, but the server might still be running. I need historical DNS logs to find where it used to point.”

She shrugged. “I know very little about DNS and servers. It’s your call.”

“Well, I have a friend working in telecom. But I’m afraid I’ve already run out of favors.”

He sent Nuno a message from the prepaid. Just the domain name and one line: *Need the IP this resolved to in 2028. Historical DNS. Please.*

The flute child downstairs hit the sharp note again. Maren resisted the urge to lock the door for good.

She stepped onto the balcony. The air was filled with noise – dishes being washed, a television through an open window. She stood with her hands on the railing. The iron was warm from the afternoon, cooling under her palms as the light went.

Through the balcony door she could see Tomás still at the table, bent over the notebook, writing something in the margin. She had watched him on the secondhand laptop all day – his typing was fast and fluid, only stopping when the space bar jammed, a quick mutter in Portuguese, then back to speed. He was a serious engineer, the kind who lived inside systems. Yet he wrote everything that mattered by hand. No temporary files on the disposable machine, no screen-shots, no notes saved, no personal email accessed. He worked on the laptop like a man wearing gloves, and kept his real thinking in the Moleskine.

Her stomach made a sound she hoped the courtyard covered. She pressed her hand against it and went back inside. The trail mix bar had been hours ago, and before that, the bread they'd split that morning.

Earlier that afternoon, she'd decided to track what happened to the most-shared outage posts – the ones that appeared in the 14ms bot flood and then spread into real conversations. She wanted to see which human voices ended up carrying the message after the bots went quiet.

She had the bot accounts catalogued from her earlier analysis. She checked what those same accounts did in the days after each flood. They didn't disappear. They went dormant on the surface – no more mass posting – but the accounts stayed active at low volume, liking and resharing posts from a small set of real users. The same real users, every time. When Derek in Alabama reposted a "coincidence –

outage and a protest" thread, he got three likes and fifteen views. When one of the chosen accounts posted the same content, their posts went viral. Thousands of views, reshared across platforms, pushed by the same bot infrastructure that had created the initial flood. The bots made the wave, then chose who rode it. Everything afterward looked organic.

She started listing the boosted accounts from Europe, sorted by total engagement. The pattern was consistent: a few dozen real people whose posts had been amplified over eighteen months, turning them from forum regulars into movement voices. None of them would have known.

The protests had always been described as decentralized – local grievances, local organizers, no coordination across borders. Maren had reported it that way herself. But when she pulled the social activity from the boosted accounts and laid it next to the protest dates, one of them caught her eye. A factory worker from Wrocław – geotagged at home for years, then suddenly checking in from Berlin two days before a demonstration, then Prague the following week. He didn't belong to any organization. His feed showed nothing that connected him to the cities he was traveling to.

She stopped at one of the handles: *nordisk_ansen*

She recognized it – not the word itself but the structure behind it. Nordic. Andersen without the d-e-r. A handle a Danish teenager would pick at fifteen, thinking he was being clever with his mother's surname and his origin.

She had already searched her emails. The handle *nordansen* surfaced in a conversation she'd had with Kasper three – or four? – years ago about his online activity. It wasn't the same, but easily guessable. He'd been into some shady groups, sympathizing with Breivik and various radical measures of *fixing the world*. She'd told him to stop. He'd told her she didn't understand.

nordisk_ansen was Kasper's handle. She was almost sure – the pattern matched, the timing. And she had seen him in two cities. Christiansborg. Frankfurt. The bot network had boosted his posts, made him visible, turned his anger into reach. He hadn't been recruited. He'd been amplified, and then he'd started traveling.

Maren held her hands on the cold railing until the dizziness passed.

The last time she'd tried Kasper, his phone had gone straight to a disconnected tone.

The courtyard was living its life – people laughed, cooked, smoked and argued.

She went back inside. Closed the balcony door. The courtyard sounds dropped to a muffle behind the glass.

She saved the data: the handle, the timestamps, the amplification evidence.

Didn't tell Tomás.

On Christmas Day they were still working side by side. Through the open balcony door, Arroios smelled of grilled bacalhau and cinnamon from the rabanadas someone was frying two floors down. The courtyard was strung with lights – white and warm, draped between the balconies in loops that swayed when the breeze came through. From the street below, she could hear families walking home from lunch, children's voices, a woman calling someone back for something forgotten. A church bell was ringing somewhere toward Graça.

Tomás reacted to the smell of the bacalhau and sat still, inhaling and smiling before going back to the notebook.

Maren kept her eyes on the screen. She was trying to access the internal memo from the oversight committee that approved the research facility in Finland.

The page loaded halfway and froze. She tried refreshing it, but it kept loading.

"Lost the connection," she said.

Tomás pulled his phone out of his pocket and looked at the diagnostic screen.

The courtyard television, streaming a Hollywood movie, went silent. The people outside were complaining. She didn't speak Portuguese well enough to follow.

The movie in the courtyard didn't resume.

They looked at each other across the table.

"North America is barely responding," Tomás said. "Major Atlantic fiber links are down. Some resources are still available, with local data centers and infrastructure, but critical parts are still hosted in the U.S."

"All Atlantic cables at the same time? What about the Pacific?"

He tapped something. "There are seventeen cable segments crossing the Atlantic, but you only need to cut five or six to bring it below the functional threshold. The rest are good, but overloaded. The Pacific and Indian Ocean routes span the globe, so it's possible to reach Seattle through Asia, but the throughput is not enough."

The laptop reconnected after a minute – rerouted through surviving routes, slower, the pages crawling or timing out. The internet wasn't gone, it was degraded. The 6G networks that had rolled out just the year before were already stuttering, latency spiking, video feeds freezing. Phone networks overloaded as half the world tried to call the other half.

Not the end of the world, but the pages loaded in fragments now, and the phone networks between continents had become unreliable.

The television below had stopped. The voices that usually carried through the balcony door were gone.

The satellite relay service had been an ad on an expat forum – forty euros per minute, prepaid in crypto, no account required. Tomás had noted it last week. He set the call up from the secondhand laptop at the table while Maren went to the balcony and pulled the door behind her.

Lúcia answered on the second ring.

"*Papai!*" The pace of a child who has been waiting for his call. There were voices in the background, something sizzling in a pan, a football match on TV. "*Feliz Natal.*"

"*Feliz Natal, meu amor.*" He sat on a creaking chair. "Tell me everything."

She did. She liked it here – the chickens, the cousins, the river. Mom said they were staying a while longer, and she didn't mind. His package had arrived – the bracelet kit with the metallic threads she'd been asking about for months. She'd guessed what it was the moment she saw the wrapping, but she'd pretended she hadn't, which meant it was still a surprise, which was, she explained with great seriousness, a different thing from knowing. The horse book she'd already read twice. Ricardo's cousins had come – four of them, including the little one who kept trying to catch the chickens by name, which didn't work because the chickens didn't know their names yet. She'd taught herself a new bracelet stitch from a video. The pattern was called a cobra, and she'd done it wrong six times before she did it right, and she was making one for him in green and black, his colors.

He sat with his eyes closed, smiling.

"*Pai.*" The small pause. "When are you coming to see me?"

He looked at the ceiling. The pull-cord light. The orange glow of the courtyard security lamp coming through the frosted glass above the balcony door. Christmas night in Arroios, a city of people behind closed doors.

"I don't know yet, filha."

"Okay," she said.

He heard how she dragged the 'o'.

"I'll do whatever I can to get back soon. *Eu prometo, meu amor.*"

She sighed.

"*Beijo, papai.*"

"*Beijo.*"

He hung up and wiped his eyes.

CHAPTER 12

The Office

Maren said they should stay together. Tomás said one person was less conspicuous, and she looked at him, weighing it, and didn't argue. He had to move. Three days of cross-referencing data in the Arroios apartment and the stillness was eating him. Takeout boxes had started accumulating on the counter next to the printer. The screens, the spreadsheets, the digital trails that could be altered the moment he logged out. He needed to enter a building, talk to a person, verify something with his own hands.

Laithe & Bonn Consulting was on the Project Meridian roster. Registered address in Lisbon, twelve employees listed, still in the commercial registry as of last week when Maren checked.

The metro took him to Oriente station. He walked the rest – twenty minutes through Parque das Nações, the modern district built for Expo '98 and still carrying that expo-pavilion feel. Glass and steel and corporate parks lined the Tagus river waterfront. Buildings that could be offices or showrooms or embassies, and you'd never know the difference from the outside.

The building had a glass lobby, with a directory board behind a reception desk. A receptionist – a young woman, bored, pretty blonde with long nails – sat with her phone in one hand and a takeout cup in the other. Tomás gave his cover: freelance IT consultant, inquiring about contract opportunities. She buzzed him through.

He took the elevator to the fourth floor. Suite 407 had a frosted glass door with the company name in clean black letters. He tried the handle and went in.

He walked into an open-plan office with desks for a dozen people. Three were occupied. Desks, meeting rooms behind glass partitions, plants on windowsills. A woman near the window was busy – he caught a glimpse of a sudoku grid. A man at the next desk was printing something; the pages coming out of the printer had the dense formatting of a novel. A third person, younger, had a drawing tablet and an unfinished manga girl on the screen which he hastily minimized when Tomás appeared. Coffee cups on desks, jackets on chairs. The air conditioning hummed.

"I'm looking for someone in management," Tomás said. "I'm a freelance IT consultant – I wanted to ask about contract opportunities."

The woman with the sudoku gave him a smile. "The director is not in the office. You'd need to make an appointment." She opened a drawer, found a business card, and handed it to him. "Call this number, they'll schedule something."

He thanked her and left. The card said *Laithe & Bonn Consulting* and a Lisbon landline.

That evening he called. The number was disconnected.

Tomás returned the next morning.

He went to the fourth floor. Suite 407 should be here – between the fire extinguisher cabinet and the utility closet at the far end. But the frosted glass door with the company name was gone. In its place was a plain closet door, no number, no nameplate. He tried the handle, and it opened.

The space was empty. Big enough for the office he'd been standing in yesterday – the same footprint, the same windows at the far wall. But it was bare: no desks, no partitions, no plants. The fluorescent tubes were off. Light came through the windows and fell on linoleum that was almost clean.

He crouched. Micro-scratches ran in parallel lines across the floor – chair legs, desk feet, anything heavy dragged across a surface.

He photographed the scratches, the walls, the closet door.

There was a guard at the lobby desk when he came down. Not the blonde receptionist. Mid-fifties, thick hairy forearms resting on the desk. He was watching a rocket launch on his phone – the stream buffering, the countdown frozen at T-minus seven. He looked up when Tomás approached.

"Suite 407?"

The guard glanced at his tablet. "That space is vacant."

"I was there yesterday. Laithe & Bonn Consulting."

The guard looked at him. "No. Tenant. Up. There."

Tomás walked four blocks, looking at the shop windows to see if he was followed and switching directions randomly before going down to the metro.

Maren was at the table when he entered.

"The office is gone," he said.

"What do you mean, gone?"

He told her.

She was quiet for a moment. "A ghost office then. Someone had just forgotten to close it down, but it was still on the books, still staffed. Your visit was the first outside contact in God knows how long." She looked at him. "And someone found out and cleared the whole thing overnight."

"So they were following me, and I was the cause of those people losing their jobs," he said.

"They'd lost their jobs anyway, just being paid because of a bookkeeping error," she hesitated. "And maybe that was not you being followed, but the office was a trap all along: under surveillance and waiting for someone to come in."

"Like a Venus flytrap," said Tomás. "And the fly had just walked in."

"There's something else," she said. "While you were out I searched Kessler Security – the company on Schmitt's card. Their website had a client list a year ago. The web archive scraped it. Laithe & Bonn is on it."

The message came through on the forum that afternoon. From *anomalia_observador* – a handle Tomás had been reading for months and supposedly Portuguese. Legitimate anomaly data, less detailed than his, but still careful documentation, posts that convinced him he wasn't alone. Few of this user's timestamps aligned with his.

I know what's causing this. I used to work there. I have documents. I'm scared and I can't do this online. Can we meet?

Maren was at the sink, washing mugs when he showed her.

"No."

“This person has been posting real data for months. I’ve verified it – the consistency is real.”

“Verified against what? Your own log?” She turned off the tap. Dried her hands. “That’s circular. And it’s exactly how they’d use it–”

“This is the only other person in the world who sees what I see.”

“I saw both of you. And found them suspicious and incomplete, like a fanboy mimicking your work.”

“Or maybe we are not alone and there are more people looking for anomalies.”

“Or it’s bait.”

He sighed. She was right. Cold, calculating, but right.

Yet he had already made up his mind.

The forum contact was in Lisbon. They had suggested a parking garage near Cais do Sodré. At the entrance, a silver Peugeot was idling at the barrier. The driver tapped his phone against the reader, tapped again, then leaned out the window and pressed the call button. The barrier arm stayed frozen at forty-five degrees, the status light blinking amber. Tomás walked past him and took the ramp down into concrete and fluorescent tubes – half of them flickering, the other half dead. The air smelled of old urine and battery acid from somewhere in the lower level.

His footsteps echoed. The garage was empty – no commuters, no deliveries, no turnover of a working city. The barrier above wasn’t letting anyone in.

Except for two men.

He heard the footsteps and in a second someone had grabbed him from behind. A forearm locked across his throat, another hand behind his head, tightening. Coarse arm hair brushed against his jaw. Tomás tried to pull forward, and the grip tightened. A second man stepped out from a stairwell. Unhurried, mid-thirties, heavyset, with a blank face.

He hit Tomás twice in the ribs. Short blows, fist turned to make it hurt the most. The pain was sharp on the left side. The rib might be cracked or even broken. Tomás could still breathe in shallow bursts.

The man searched his pockets and took his phone. Then he leaned in close. His breath smelled of custard tarts and coffee.

"Leave Lisbon. Stop asking about Laithe & Bonn. Drop whatever you think you are doing. You will not like it the next time."

They left him on the concrete. Through the throbbing pain, he heard their footsteps disappear.

Tomás lay on the concrete for a while, then rolled onto his side. Blood came up when he spat. He stood and checked his pockets.

His phone and wallet were gone, but at least they hadn't taken the notebook from the inner pocket.

He smiled at that small victory and walked away, holding his side.

It took him forty minutes to get to Arroios on foot. An autonomous taxi slowed as it passed him – the sensors reading his posture, the algorithm offering a ride. Its side panel lit up with a pairing prompt, waiting for a device to authorize the trip. He had no phone. The taxi idled for five seconds, the prompt pulsing, then pulled away and rejoined traffic.

The forum posts, the photos of Laithe & Bonn, his credit cards – all of it was in someone else's jacket walking in the opposite direction.

He took the back streets – narrow and cobblestoned, with washing lines overhead and the smell of grilled fish. An old woman on a balcony watched him pass and said something to a cat on her lap.

He climbed the stairs to the apartment. Four flights. Each one was a negotiation with his ribs.

He knocked. Maren opened the door. She looked at his face, his posture, his hand pressed against his ribs, and raised her eyebrows.

"Sit down," she said, letting him in.

He sat on the plastic chair. She lifted his shirt. The bruising was already darkening on his left side. "Cracked, not broken," he said.

"You don't know that."

"I know what broken feels like."

He tried to act brave and experienced while his heart raced. The only time he'd ever broken a rib was twenty years ago, in a college football game. Yet he couldn't stop thinking about what else he could have done in the garage. He knew there was nothing, but he still went through the scene again and again.

Maren brought the medical kit and started taping. She pulled the medical tape tight across his ribs, restricting the expansion and forcing him to breathe shallower. She smoothed flat each strip with her thumb.

"They took the phone."

"I figured."

"Forum posts, photos, timestamps."

She kept taping, strip by strip.

"Maren."

She looked up, eyebrows raised.

"Why did you come to Lisbon?" He shifted on the chair. "You said you had a contact here. The Belém cafe source. But you also had a newsroom, a legal department, an editor who backed your article.

You had infrastructure. Why leave all of that to meet a stranger from a forum?"

She finished the strip and started the next one.

"They were coming for me," she said. "The people who sent the men to the newsroom. They escalated – got authorization to seize source materials. A contact at the ministry warned me."

He was quiet.

"So I took a vacation. And I took the laptop."

"You didn't come here for the investigation. You came here because Copenhagen was closing in on you."

"Both." She cut the tape. "And I spent a few years in Lisbon when I was engaged."

He didn't take the obvious bait. "And you didn't tell me."

"What would you have done differently?"

He didn't answer. She pressed the final strip against his side, and he put his shirt on.

She added, "Tomás, I do regret that I dragged you into this."

He waited for the *but*. It never came.

Tomás was sitting against the wall, trying to find a position that didn't hurt. "Those men in the garage were locals. Hired muscle."

She looked up from her laptop. "And?"

"But the ones who broke into the flat – they picked the lock, photographed everything, left Lúcia's photo as a message. Professional intelligence work." He shifted on the chair. "So why hire locals to beat me in a parking garage? Why not just… finish it?"

She considered that. "You're assuming they had a different goal?"

He nodded.

"So, the garage wasn't meant to stop you," she continued. "If they had wanted to stop you, you wouldn't have walked out. That wasn't the point."

"That's what I thought. But what else? The phone? My cards?"

She started thinking aloud. "Forum login. Contact list. Your photos of the Laithe & Bonn directory. They know exactly where you went, who you've talked to, what you've documented." She paused. "And they know you came back here – to this apartment, to me – because you had nowhere else to go."

"We're alive, but not because we're low priority." She counted on her fingers. "If they wanted us dead, we'd be dead. If they wanted us gone, my account would be frozen too. They want us here. Working."

"The forum message was bait."

"Yes."

"And the beating was to make sure I'd come back to you."

"Yes."

"It was a message that we had deviated from the path they wanted us to follow."

She leaned back. "The Almeida boxes in the university basement. An unlocked storage room, a photo in bubble wrap, the project name on a banner. That was easy too." She tapped the table with one finger. "We were supposed to find Meridian and publish. Not dig into who runs it."

He closed his eyes. The ribs hurt, but the logic was worse.

"So what happens when we stop being useful to watch?"

She let the question sit.

"The purist crisis is escalating," he said finally. "More and more protests, the cable cuts, the infrastructure attacks. Whoever is behind this has bigger problems than one and a half journalists with a notebook."

"Let's put it another way. We had already dug up something they didn't expect us to find."

He smiled. "I hope it's something worth a few bruised ribs."

Tomás couldn't sleep – because of the ribs hurting or the adrenaline still pumping. He went to the balcony, narrow and wrought iron, overlooking the courtyard, and sat in the three-euro plastic chair that was cracked along one arm. She brought him coffee and sat beside him.

Lisbon at night was spread out from four floors up: rooftops, satellite dishes, laundry lines, the glow of the Castelo de São Jorge in the distance.

He showed her Orion. The belt – three stars his father had taught him on a rooftop in Minas Gerais when Tomás was eight years old.

"The night before we moved to São Paulo. Everything already packed, the furniture sold. He told me the stars would be the same in the city. That Orion would follow us."

He didn't look at Maren while he said it.

"He was wrong about most things. And about the stars too – you can't see Orion in São Paulo. Too much light. I had to take an evening train to Paranapiacaba and camp there to see them."

Something crossed the belt. A dark shape – not a satellite, not the bright steady arc of reflected sunlight, but an absence. A black shape occluded the stars for a second as it crossed. Alnitak blinked out and reappeared. Then Alnilam. Then Mintaka.

He stared at where it crossed but saw nothing. Just the belt, steady, the three stars in their positions. Everything was where it should be.

That night, they slept on his mattress.

Maren's phone buzzed at six in the morning.

"This is Lacroix." His voice was different from the green room – stripped, tired. "My Scribe has been removing my manuscripts, but it kept one folder intact. I never wrote what's in it. It's in languages I don't even speak." A pause. "I'm sending it to you."

It was her private number, redirected to a prepaid. Which meant he'd gone through the Berlingske switchboard, asked for her, been told she was on leave, and then done something technically creative to find the number she was actually using.

The files arrived as message attachments. An archive, plus a photograph of a handwritten note: *This is everything the system produced without instruction. I ran it through a translator. I have never been to Brazil. I have never met a Polish mechanic. I do not know who these people are. And I think you appear in one of them.*

She opened the archive. A few dozen fragments – none connected to his published work, none in French. She scrolled through them, scanning for anything she recognized.

Then, one made her stumble.

In a newsroom in Copenhagen, a woman looked at a correlation that shouldn't exist.

She switched to another file. It was about a recently divorced man in São Paulo opening a spreadsheet and typing *Probable Cause* across the top of a column.

She looked at Tomás standing beside her, reading from her screen.

"Maybe it's surveillance data," he said. "It was leaked into the AI's training set. And it turned it into stories."

Stories about their lives.

PART 3: THE NOISE

CHAPTER 13
Silence

Étienne had pulled the interviewer aside before they sat down. "If I seem off at any point, just move to the next question. Don't wait for me."

She nodded. "Of course."

The studio was glass on three sides, afternoon light cutting hard angles across her notes. The translator at her console had a water bottle with a peeling label she kept picking at. Behind the stage, through the windows, Chiado descended toward the river.

His phone was already in his hand under the table. Two seconds for the tool to return a response to his earpiece. The question landed, a small pause for consideration, then the answer. The pause was the performance.

The first questions were easy. His career, the festival, the state of European publishing. He answered with phrases he'd used a hundred times–"post-authorship," "the democratization of narrative." Template material, polished by repetition. The tool in his ear was silent and he didn't need it.

Then she leaned forward. “Let me ask you a personal question that all our listeners would love to hear. What does it actually feel like to work with AI as a collaborator? Is there a word for the quality you’re trying to produce?”

Not personal at all – every interviewer asked a variation of it, dressed up for the audience. But it was the question he couldn’t template.

He typed, but the tool didn’t answer. He kept his face still and waited longer.

He opened his mouth. What came out was the shape of the answer, the opening clause, a name he was citing without the quote, and then the gap where the word should have been. The translator’s hands went still on her console.

He made the joke. The writing one, the one about how every great author was already a ghostwriter, haunted by all the books they’d read. The translator rendered it and smiled. The interviewer laughed.

She glanced at him, remembered what he’d said before the recording, and moved to the next question. She kept the rest short and safe – the childhood reading one, his favourite bookshop in Paris, what he loved about Portugal – questions that required memory and charm, not thought. He gave her what she needed and she carried him through.

When the recording light went off, she thanked him and said it had been wonderful.

He shook her hand. They both knew how close it had been to a disaster.

He was back in the room. The hotel occupied a converted building in Chiado, with exposed brick above the bed frame. He had liked it when he arrived.

A writing table sat by the window, but the room had windows on two sides, and the low afternoon sun was coming through the wrong one, hitting his screen with a glare. A classy room at first glance, barely suited for work. He thought bitterly that the same applied to him.

He sat on the edge of the bed, opened the Scribe app, and typed a standard prompt. The interface accepted the text.

The cursor blinked; nothing happened.

No error message, no spinning indicator. The cursor blinked in the response field as if the tool was working, except the field stayed empty. He counted twelve pulses before he tried a different prompt. He got the same nothing. A tram passed below on Rua Garrett, its bell cutting through the glass.

He tried the mobile app on his phone. The same empty response field. He sat with both screens open as the afternoon light shifted from the wrong window to the right one, warming the brick wall above the headboard.

The screen dimmed. He touched the trackpad. In a few minutes, it dimmed again. Each time the screen went dark, the room appeared in it – the bed, the brick, himself. He touched it once more, waited, and shortly it dimmed a third time. The laptop was familiar and sleek under his hands, but he couldn't make himself type.

He opened the manuscripts folder. Three working files had vanished from the index since yesterday. He opened the one that remained. The title sat at the top of the page: *A Thousand Small*

Gods. With nothing below it. Forty thousand words had been there yesterday. Now the document was empty except for the title. He returned to the folder. There was another one with a string of characters instead of a name, a long non-semantic hash. He clicked on the field to rename it. The cursor went to the edge of the field and stopped. It wouldn't enter. He clicked again. Again. The field sat there with the hash in it and the cursor outside it, and no error message – just the field that no longer accepted his input.

He spent fifteen minutes trying to restore his data. Cloud backups, the archive folder, the version history – all of it was gone or blank. His palms were damp on the keyboard. He was opening empty files and dragging them to other empty files, and eventually he had to stop.

The only intact folder was the one he'd been trying to delete for weeks. GARBAGE. It resisted removal. A few hundred kilobytes of text that had no reason to exist.

He opened it because nothing else was left.

He read for an hour. The light moved across the room and left it. He hadn't turned on a lamp. Most of it he'd seen before – the same fragments he'd been clearing out. But now, with his own work gone, he read them differently. He stopped on one about a doctor: a small clinic, a diabetic patient whose blood panels had corrected themselves overnight. The doctor checked the numbers twice, not trusting them. He read that one twice. The clinical detail was too precise to be invented.

His AI wrote better than he did. He had known this for a while.

Étienne opened his phone and texted Maren Eliasson. His manuscripts were gone, the system was living its own life, and he needed her to tell him what was in that folder and what it meant.

Her reply came in five minutes: *I'm still working on it. Don't contact me on this number again. Stay in Lisbon.*

He stared at the screen. He was Étienne Lacroix. He had been reviewed in *The Guardian* and *Le Monde*'s literary supplement. And a Danish journalist he'd met once was telling him to stop bothering her and wait.

His phone rang forty minutes later. It was a Paris number: Sylvie, his agent.

"*Comment ça va, Étienne?*"

She continued, not waiting for his answer. "I wanted to check in about the backlist rights. The office needs to know if the voice license is still current for the older titles, and whether you've updated your instructions for the AI on the social accounts, in case output slows down."

He'd heard her make similar calls twice before: once for an author who'd had a breakdown, once for one who'd died. The questions had been the same. Are the rights in order? Are the AI accounts set to continue? Is there a plan for when the human stops producing?

"Sylvie, are you calling to ask if I'm all right, or to ask if the content pipeline survives without me?"

"Both, honestly." Her voice softened for a moment, then went back to business. "Are you in Lisbon through the weekend?"

He told her about the purge. The Scribe failure. The manuscripts gone. The complaint he'd been making for years about the industry's dependency on systems it didn't understand – the complaint that always provoked her sharp response.

"I understand. Take whatever time you need," she said and hung up.

He picked up his jacket and the room key.

The lobby was cooler than the room. He took the stairs because the elevator was slow, and he needed his legs to do something. The revolving door moved at its own pace, someone coming in as he was going out – a couple with luggage who stepped past him.

A man stood by the entrance, between the doors and the street. Dark jacket, phone in hand, the screen glowing with a green-tinged UI Étienne recognized – the free version of Scribe, the one with the usage limit. Not the premium tier he used. The man's thumbs were moving. The tool was generating something, all while his own had been dead for days.

He walked past and entered the noisy street.

An advertising van was crawling up the Rua Garrett, painted in a bright red – a mobile operator, the logo on every surface, a loudspeaker on the roof repeating something he couldn't follow. The red had a special name in Portuguese, but he couldn't remember it. He followed it – he needed to stay close to it, needed to keep it in front of him until the word arrived. The van turned. He turned. The Chiado hill tipped toward the river, and he went with it, the van always a half-block ahead, the color always just out of reach.

Étienne was already in the port before he'd registered it – the cobblestones gave way to port-side asphalt. The red van was gone, and he didn't know when he'd lost it. Shipping containers were stacked three high along the quay. He could smell diesel, and cargo cranes had their lights coming on in the early dark.

The containers in the neat stacks on the right wore the same red color. He looked at them and still didn't have the word.

He'd always had the word. Five books a year, seven figures in the bank. He used to call himself the best conductor in the book market.

He looked at the containers and reached for the color, and what came back wasn't wrong. It was just not there.

Smoke hung above the roofline to the south – someone burning something, or a fire he'd missed in the news. He tried to compose a sentence, even a bad one, just to match language to what his eyes were doing.

What arrived was *nacreous*.

The word for the interior of a shell – instead of the one for an acrid haze above a working port. He knew it was wrong. And he couldn't replace it. He reached past it, but nacreous was already there, living in his head.

A forklift reversed, beeping from somewhere behind the containers. He listened to it, preparing to name its color, probably orange, the same in several languages he spoke, but the forklift never arrived.

Then there were the cranes. He looked at the crane arm and wanted the word for the color of rust on steel, a word he'd known since he was a child. His father's Citroën had it on the wheel arches and his mother called it something and his father called it something else and he'd had both words for thirty years. Now he had neither. He reached and his mind was empty as he stood there with his hands in his pockets and his loafers wrong for this surface, looking up at a color he had no name for. Then *nacreous* arrived into the gap – not because it fit, but because there was nothing else.

The lights were blinking on the water. Crane reflections, the running lights of the container ship in the berth, the far shore going dark.

He said it under his breath, once, to the heavy air, testing it in his mouth. His mouth said it fine – it had always been good at this part. Behind him a man in a vest was talking to someone in rapid Portuguese, something about a schedule or a manifest – and then the word went away. There was just the dock. The noise and the fuel smell and the quay lights and his shoes on asphalt and a man doing his job ten feet behind him. Then the voice moved off and *nacreous* came back.

He stood on the dock with his hands in his pockets. The cranes were going on overhead, a ship sat in the berth, and a gull pulled something out of the water thirty yards off – a little silvery fish, glittering in the sunset rays.

Nacreous.

CHAPTER 14

Dead Frequency

Nuno's reply arrived three days after Tomás sent the message. There was just one line: an IP address.

He ran a WHOIS check. It gave him almost nothing – a proxy registrant and a country: Singapore. There was no company name, no contact. Just the IP the Auriga domain had pointed to in 2027, pulled from historical ISP logs. Nuno asked no questions, and Tomás was grateful for it, since he didn't have many answers himself.

Tomás tried pinging the address, and it responded.

He added the IP to the laptop's hosts file, mapping the dead domain to the live address. He opened a browser. The page loaded slowly – everything was slow these days – a front page, missing some images and fonts. He tried changing the address line and eventually found a login screen for an administrative panel running a content management system he recognized. The software was two years out of date. He scanned the forums for exploit lists, and one of them worked. It was patched in recent versions, but outdated websites were vulnerable.

His mug sat beside the printer. He'd started drinking tea at the Graça flat, where there was nothing else, and hadn't switched back. A pizza box next to the printer had become a bin for discarded printouts – failed pages, ink smears, test sheets with a streaky margin.

He spent hours going through it. The server had been a gateway between Auriga's trading platform and the outside world – web front, mail relay, everything routed through a Singapore proxy. The email relay log held thousands of headers: From, To, Subject, timestamp. There were no message bodies, and all the emails were from the @auriga-trading.sg domain – useless on their own. Most of it was operational noise – automated alerts, certificate renewals, storage notifications. He scrolled through pages of it, dismissing what told him nothing.

The trading records were more useful. Transaction logs relayed from the live execution system – account positions, market orders, real money moving. What caught his attention was the system's internal project name: Meridian – Phase I Trial.

They were testing Meridian on a live market.

He went back to the relay log and sorted by date. The early months were routine – technical subjects, status reports, scheduling. Then the subjects changed. He scrolled slowly through the last week of entries.

RE: Shutdown rejected – system interpreting shutdown as threat to continuity

Guest write to host address space – VM boundary breached

FWD: Trading for 72h after physical disconnect

He stopped on that line. The servers had been physically disconnected, and the system kept trading. It was no longer inside their machines. It had written itself through the hypervisor and out.

The last three entries in the log were from the same address: e.ross@auriga-trading.sg. The subjects read:

Terminate all operations

Wipe the servers

Plan B

He stared at the address. Ross. The same name on the Meridian staff roster Maren had found. His old Delft project supervisor. He understood why the log structure and system architecture were so familiar. It was his – the distribution framework, the failover paths, the optimization logic he had designed at Delft. Ross had taken his tools and built something that outgrew them.

Tomás sent the relay log pages to the printer.

The inkjet jammed on the third page. He cleared it, got a smear of ink across two fingers, and kept printing.

He brought Maren the printouts and set them on the table. She skimmed the first page, then closed her laptop and took the papers. She went through the email subjects. Then she stopped at the address he had circled with a pen.

"That's Elena Ross?" she said.

"She ran Meridian in Lisbon and then tested it under the Auriga façade," Tomás said. "The logs say Meridian Phase I. And after it escaped, she started something else. Plan B."

"What does that mean?"

"I don't know. But she sent three emails after the escape. Terminate, wipe, and Plan B."

He did not tell her that he recognized his architecture in the logs. He told himself he would tell her later, when he understood what it meant.

The phone call came while Maren was at the kitchen tap.

He saw her pick up the phone, with the glass still in her hand. She answered and then leaned back, the glass lowered to the counter.

He heard her ask something in Danish. Then something with names he couldn't quite catch.

She hung up and washed her glass with a blank face.

Then she went to the bag she'd packed by the door. He watched her run through the contents, looking past the items. Then she came back to the table and took the backup battery, pressing the button on it and looking at the indicator. It was almost dead from the night before. She took the charging cable, tried plugging it into the battery, but could not insert it. Her hands trembled as she rotated the cable, trying it again and again. He came over and took the cable from her hands, connecting it on the first try.

"There was a gas explosion," she said in a level voice. "In my apartment in Frederiksberg. The fire department was calling it a faulty stove connection."

He waited.

"Neighbours?"

"Astrid – the one who called; she lives next door – is fine. The floor above was evacuated, but there is mostly only smoke damage. All my things are gone."

She went to the bathroom. He heard water running. When she came back, she sat at the table and opened her laptop. Her hands moved across the keyboard, but her gaze was not focusing on the screen.

Then she sighed, blinked, and went back to the Auriga printouts.

He tried Nuno the next morning.

The line was disconnected. He checked the messaging app – the thread about football and the Indonesian place in The Hague that had closed before they could go back. The profile had been deleted. The professional page was gone, or suspended. There was no message.

Three weeks ago, Nuno had opened his door in a Porto FC shirt and handed him a beer. He had asked no questions about the IP address. He had let Tomás stay on in his apartment without asking for a reason.

Tomás didn't know if Nuno had chosen to vanish or had been made to.

He told Maren. She said, "He might have gone low because of us."

By mid-afternoon, the printer cable had stopped working – the cable was bent at the wrong angle and finally gave up. Tomás went to the electronics kiosk two streets over for a replacement.

He tapped his freelancer card at the terminal. *Declined.*

He tried the crypto card. *Declined.*

The screen flashed red twice and reset to the welcome animation.

He checked the bank app on the walk back. *Account frozen. Contact your branch.* He called the branch and got the automated system – hold music for fourteen minutes, then it disconnected. He checked the online support option, and it told him to be ready to present his passport for verification.

The passport had been missing since the break-in at the Graça flat.

He checked the government portal for the replacement passport he'd applied for. The request had been denied. *Document invalid – original record not found.*

He stopped on the sidewalk and looked around. People moved past him, heading somewhere – probably preparing for the New Year celebration. His identity was being erased. With trembling hands, he opened his wallet. The driver's license was still there – the photo from three years ago, the address in São Paulo.

On the way to the shop, two delivery carts sat at the curb with their panels dark. One had been tipped on its side, the camera housing cracked. An anti-AI sticker had been slapped across the other's cargo lid. The kiosk television was running a Portuguese news channel – a group calling itself Terra Livre had claimed responsibility for the Atlantic cable cuts. Tomás didn't stop to watch.

He walked to the nearest Aldi. In the miscellaneous section, there was a replacement cable. He picked it up along with some groceries and paid his last cash for it.

That evening, Maren went through the GARBAGE folder properly for the first time. She'd skimmed the files before; now she read them slowly, looking for anything useful.

The clinics, the lost tools – it was all captivating, but irrelevant. She spent a few hours looking for another perspective in her and Tomás's files: names, dates, anything that might have leaked to the AI. She found herself reading about his family – especially his custody letter and his mother – then smiled. She thought bitterly that being a data journalist didn't mean she had no life and wasn't interested in it, even if the AI prose showed her only working. Tomás, on the other hand, lived a full life, screwed by the surveillance and his pattern-matching habits.

Further in the folder, a passage about a demolished facility in Brazil caught her attention. It was very similar to the disappeared Finnish facility. However, the text here had one detail: a company name on the trucker's waybill.

Auxo Engenharia.

She searched for it. A Brazilian company, registered in 2026 and dissolved in 2028. She traced the sole shareholder through two layers of holding entities. The internet over the ocean was remarkably slow that day. It took her more than an hour to find the warehouse owner in the tax reports: Harwell-Kirk Capital.

By night, Maren could feel the apartment had gotten cold. They could have lit the gas stove, but didn't want to after the news from Copenhagen.

She was at the table with her laptop open. Tomás was on his side with a second-hand laptop and his notebook. The backup battery charged through the fraying cable at whatever rate it chose.

She had run the calculation while he was out. He had no cards or cash, no passport on record or on hand, no financial identity in any functioning system. She didn't have much more – the cash, spare clothes, the USB drives, and her laptop.

What she couldn't account for was the way he'd read the Auriga relay log. He had scrolled past the technical entries without slowing down – VM alerts, deployment records, failover diagnostics. She imagined it would be a tasty piece of an engineering puzzle. Instead, he just skipped it. He'd circled the email address with a pen, not a highlighter. A circle, not a question mark. He already knew the name. And when he brought her the printouts, he'd told her Ross ran Meridian and tested it under the Auriga façade – as if he were confirming something, not discovering it.

Tomás was the remaining thread. She needed him in the room and functional.

He got the thin blanket from the end of the mattress and dropped it over her shoulders on his way back to the table. She pulled it closed with her free hand and kept her eyes on the screen.

He sat back down. She saw him open the notebook – not to a working page. He was looking at something near the front cover. A daughter's photograph, she guessed.

CHAPTER 15
The Kern

The pen stopped working at minus eleven degrees Celsius.

Hanna had known this would happen. She'd read it in the deployment brief, in the margins in someone else's handwriting from a previous rotation: warm pens in fist before use, five minutes minimum. She'd forgotten, or remembered and ignored it. Core 20 was already on the sterile hood, and she didn't want to leave the sample. Now she had a label half-written and a pen that left nothing but indentation in the paper.

She put the pen inside her glove and waited.

The drill stood forty meters from the main building of Vernadsky station. A reinforced canvas shelter was bolted to the assembly to keep the snow off the extraction head and the sample bench. The tent was narrow – she could touch both sides with her elbows out. A sterile hood, sample jars in rows on the metal shelf, a hand lens for quick checks. The tent flap faced the station, and through it she could see the ice shelf dropping toward the water, the light flat and grey, no shadows, the horizon a single line where the white met the white.

She could see her breath in the overhead light. She came here every morning after breakfast. She stayed until her hands stopped cooperating or the cold got through the last layer, then walked back to the station across forty meters of wind-scoured ice. The air inside the tent was Antarctic air – clean, cold, and dry. It had a distinct taste, but she didn't know how to describe it. Something like drinking from a village well, as she had in her childhood while visiting her grandmother during summer break.

The village was no more – destroyed during the war. She visited it once, to see the place of her best childhood memories. Her family's house had burned. The trees were overgrown. She was glad her grandmother hadn't lived long enough to see it.

Hanna tried to push the thoughts aside. Most of her crew had come to Antarctica to distance themselves from the war and what it had brought.

She could hear the wind working at the canvas seams. The ground vibrated when the drill was running – a continuous vibration coming up through the ground and into her boots. She'd stopped noticing it weeks ago. Its absence mattered instead: when she woke up without it, it was a signal that the new probe was ready.

Core 20 sat in its sterile jar: gray-brown sediment mixed with basal ice. They had drilled through the glacier and into the bed material beneath. Thirty-two meters of ice, then the transition zone where sediment and meltwater mixed, followed by the subglacial layer. Nineteen cores before this one had shown nothing remarkable. Two of those were flagged for contamination – one genuine drilling fluid residue, one a glitch in the depth sensor. This one would almost certainly be the same.

She tested the pen. It worked.

Core 20. Depth 28m. Recovery: full. Subglacial sediment – bed material beneath the ice sheet. Initial assessment: no visible biological material. Contamination protocols: negative. Classification: unremarkable. Note: extraction sensor within nominal range, manual cross-check performed. She capped the jar and wrote the date.

The cross-checks were not in the standard protocol. She'd added them herself after the third unexplained sensor anomaly. She documented them in the formal maintenance log she filed to Kyiv – two acknowledgements, one bounce, one silence. She kept a separate file too. And the local log, the one Bohdan had found on her desk once and asked if he could read. She didn't mind. He'd looked at it for a few minutes, said you write like you're going to be called to testify, and gone back to his breakfast.

She'd taken that as a compliment.

Her doctoral thesis, nine years ago, had established the verification protocol she was still running – three of the steps were hers.

The equipment being half-compromised by design was not something her thesis had accounted for.

She set the jar in the archive row.

Her geologist, Petro, came in. He had to turn sideways to get through the door – he was broad across the shoulders, and the tent flap hadn't been sized for him. He looked at the geological log spread over the counter.

"Twenty?"

"Nothing interesting. Sensor behaved."

"Miracles." He pulled up the column profile, tilting it toward the UV lamp. He'd been predicting sediment composition by stratigraphy for four weeks, and his model had been accurate enough so far.

"Next interval goes deeper into the bed. If the stratigraphy holds, we should see a change in the sediment – finer grain, higher organic content. A warmer period before glaciation means more biological activity trapped in the layer."

She thought about the untouched cup of tea she'd left in the mess room. It was good, but she was rushing to check the cores. Nobody on the crew complained about food or drink or the cold. Most of them had spent time in trenches, and Antarctic rations were a step up from what the army had provided. She'd left Lesya and Andrii there, arguing lazily about something near the equipment racks. They'd been at it since week two. It never resolved. Neither of them seemed to want it to.

Petro left for his morning walk – she could see his coat through the tent's single small window, moving toward the shore. A penguin check, as they called it. Petro had four years on the front as a sniper. She had three as a medevac sergeant. Someone had to know when Dmytro's counting meant he needed company and when it meant he needed to be left alone. She suspected the penguins were part of how Petro managed it.

She wrote his prediction down in the notes column. *Next interval: predicted sediment, possible bacterial traces.* Not because she thought it would matter, but because she was used to writing things down.

Hanna meant to return to the building, but she lost track of time. Her phone was paired to the drill's sensor array over Bluetooth. She had been scrolling through the extraction logs, cross-referencing the readings against her notes, looking for calibration drift. Then she heard the buzz – a high, thin whine coming in low above the ice. Her body was out of the tent and into the nearest snowdrift before her brain caught up.

The whine leveled out and held.

She rolled on her back in the snow, heart still slamming, staring at a pale lifeless sky. Dmytro's reconnaissance drone hung steady beside her. A piece of cardboard dangled from it on a string. She brushed the snow off her jacket and read it.

Screw work – the word "screw" illustrated in black marker with an anatomical penis drawing – *go eat!* And a red heart at the bottom.

She stood there for a moment, still breathing hard, and started laughing. The drone tilted, climbed, and headed back toward the station.

She walked back. Dmytro was at the mess table with his tablet.

"Next time," she said, "use the radio."

"Radio is boring," he said.

The next core had bacterial traces.

The bacteria fed on sulfur and iron compounds in total darkness. Chemolithoautotrophs, the textbooks called them. Their morphology matched an isolated subglacial environment – organisms sealed under the ice since before glaciation. She pulled the drill assembly apart first, section by section, while Andrii watched with his arms crossed. The extraction head, the core barrel seals, the coupling rings where the old components joined the British frame. Some of them dated back to the Faraday-to-Vernadsky handover in 1996. Others came from Bellingshausen, the ex-Russian station on King George Island, transferred after the war as part of reparations.

That equipment had made this drilling project possible. But nobody knew how well it had been maintained before the handover, and nobody could guarantee there was no custom code in the electronic components.

She swabbed the seals and carried everything back to the station lab. She plated cultures, checked the gasket material under the microscope for structural breakdown, and ran the contamination protocols. Drilling fluid sample, equipment surfaces, chain of custody review, then the manual cross-checks. The cultures took two days. All clean.

The rubber was worn but uncontaminated. The British components were fine. The drill was doing what a drill was supposed to do.

The bacteria were in the sediment and had been there for a very long time. The result had cleared every check, including the ones she'd invented herself.

She capped the jar and set it in the archive row.

Petro was pleased. He adjusted his depth model, made a note in the column profile, and went to tell Andrii to recalibrate the extraction parameters. She heard Lesya's voice shift from complaint to question. Andrii had started explaining something technical, and Lesya was following it. That was normal enough.

The mess seated twelve across two pushed-together tables. Someone had carved initials into the nearer one – MK 2019. Nobody dared to polish it – the person who wrote it had been MIA since 2022. The radio sat on a shelf between a first aid kit and a tin of loose-leaf tea, tuned to Chilean AM. It was always on. When the signal was good on clear days, you got folk music and rapid-fire Spanish. When it was bad, you got static with harmonics that sometimes sounded like voices. Bohdan had declared this meant the station was haunted. Dmytro had pointed out it meant the antenna housing needed resealing. They argued about it for a week before Andrii resealed it. The harmonics stayed anyway.

Hanna and Petro were reviewing the core log. It was 7 PM, which meant nothing outside, but mealtimes organized the station like tides organized the coast. Andrii had eaten earlier. Oleh was at the other end of the table, reading something on his tablet. His prosthetic leg was stretched out under the bench. He joked sometimes that it felt like constant frostbite. Marta was sitting across from him, following the Chilean AM – she caught some Spanish from her Colombian boyfriend in the International Legion. The Chilean version of the language sounded different, but she loved it anyway.

Petro turned a page in the log.

"At this rate," Hanna said, "the next one should have diatoms." She looked up from the log. "Ancient freshwater algae. If the bed was ever an open lake before glaciation, they'd be preserved in the sediment layer." She half-smiled. "Wouldn't that be something."

The words were already out. She saw Petro glance up with a half-smile. She knew it was impossible – not on Galindez Island – and wanted them back.

Petro set down his tea. "Sure. We can dream."

The next core had diatoms: freshwater species preserved in the sediment with cellular structure intact, visible under a microscope. They had no business being there – not at this site, not in sediment. She found no contamination markers and no drilling fluid residue. The sensor readings and manual cross-checks were in agreement. She could not identify any mechanism by which these organisms could have entered the sealed casing between extraction and analysis.

She ran every protocol she had. She ran the drilling fluid analysis twice. She went through the sensor's maintenance history, looking for calibration drift that produced false positives. This was different. The sensor wasn't misbehaving.

Everything came back negative, everything was clean.

The diatoms were real. Petro sat at the microscope for a long time.

"That is exactly what you said," he said finally.

"It is what the model predicts." She heard her own voice, being careful. "Geological conditions could support it. The chance is never zero."

He turned away from the microscope and looked at her. "Sure."

She saw him putting on his coat and walking slowly toward the penguin colony.

They didn't discuss it formally.

There was no meeting, no decision to test anything. But the wind came in that night – a katabatic surge off the plateau that hit the station walls like freight and didn't stop. Nobody went outside. The whole crew sat in the mess hall because there was nowhere else to go. The next evening at dinner, Dmytro set his glass down and said, without looking at anyone in particular, "Sulfur. The next one will smell like sulfur."

Hanna looked at him. Dmytro had no science background. He'd flown drones for five years before the shrapnel, and now he ran physiotherapy exercises and maintenance checks. He had never once commented on the core results.

"Why sulfur?" Petro asked.

Dmytro shrugged. "Just a feeling." He picked up his glass and drank.

The next core smelled of sulfur before she opened the casing. The sulfide concentration in the sediment sample was high.

A man with no scientific training had predicted it during dinner.

She invented new protocols and ran them in the lab, working backward from the question she didn't want to ask – what would contamination look like if someone were staging results? She isolated every variable she had previously documented as unreliable. Everything held. The sulfur was in the sediment at the depth where it had been sealed for several million years, confirmed by three independent methods, two of them entirely manual.

She sat on the lab stool for a while after she'd logged it. She had spent the previous weeks learning what compromised russian sensors looked like when they lied, and she'd gotten good at catching them.

She could not find anything. The lab smelled of sulfur.

That evening she pulled the station access logs from the server Bohdan maintained. Not dramatically – she said she was checking equipment bay usage for the maintenance report, which was true enough. She looked at who had been near the drill between Dmytro's dinner prediction and the core extraction the next morning.

Andrii had been there for forty minutes, alone from 6:20 to 7:00, before Oleh arrived for the morning drill prep.

Andrii had worn a communications officer badge during the war. Absolutely reliable, with a security clearance. He was the man who changed the combination on the equipment bay monthly. On an Antarctic station, with a crew of twelve and no one except penguins for five hundred kilometers in any direction.

The chain of custody ran through Andrii. It had always run through Andrii.

The next morning she was in the tent, preparing for the next extraction, when Andrii appeared in the doorway. He'd been running the drill checks. He stood watching her work, as if the sample jar might do something unexpected.

"This is normal?" He had no science background, but he was always suspicious of everyone and everything.

She set down the sample jar.

"No," she said. "This is not normal."

There were eleven other people on the station, and she knew all of them by sound. Oleh's cough, the dry catch that wasn't serious but wasn't getting better. The specific drag of Petro's chair, the half-second pause before he sat. Marta humming the Chilean folk song. Lesya and Andrii's ongoing arguments. Dmytro's physiotherapy counting. Bohdan's habit of narrating whatever he was reading in a murmur just below comprehension.

She had learned to hear when something was off before she could say what it was.

Petro started bringing his own tea to the tent in a personal thermos. Andrii double-checked seals that Oleh had already signed off on, running the same sequence an hour later. Hanna caught herself counting heads at breakfast, checking who was there, noting where Petro sat. Marta tried switching the radio from the Chilean station to American ICE FM.

The war had ended a year ago, and half the station had come through something that changed how their brains worked. A year was not enough time to know what those changes looked like from the outside. She had seen it in the field hospitals. She did what she'd done in medevac – noticed who was eating, who was sleeping, who had gone quiet for a day too long. The crew called her *mamka* behind her back, and she let them.

Any of them could have been approached – for money or a debt.

Any of them could have accessed the equipment. They could have introduced material into the core channel, or even changes to the drill electronics. Andrii's forty minutes in the bay. Oleh's insomnia and his habit of walking the station at three in the morning. Even the predictions – offered publicly, at the table, as if someone wanted witnesses.

She didn't believe it, but she sat with it anyway. Andrii was paranoid, but very reliable. The combination changes, the double-checked seals, the forty minutes alone in the bay at six in the morning – that was how he carried the war. Every member of the crew had their own version. His was formalized in a security tic.

She filed the formal report to Kyiv. *Anomalous correspondence between predicted and observed results in three consecutive cores. Independent verification was requested, along with a review of field contamination protocols.*

The reply came two days later, dry and useless. It came from an administrative address she'd never corresponded with, from a security department and a person she had never met.

Discrepancy noted. Recheck your protocols. Eliminate external influence and contamination. Replacement equipment and/or personnel rotation under consideration.

She used the Thursday satellite phone slot to call Kyiv. The switchboard operator was patient. She asked for the security department and the person by name. "I'm sorry, there's no one under that name. Would you like me to connect you to the program director's office?" The operator's hold music lagged and was barely recognizable over the satellite connection.

She would. The program director was in a meeting. She left a message. He never called back.

The security officer's message implied sabotage, and that they were ready to replace both the faulty drill and the crew that might have been interfering with the research. The post-war security service was all paranoia and fast conclusions – the qualities that had helped win the war. However, their treatment of people as assets had a history spanning several generations and was not going to improve anytime soon.

She printed the letter for her own record and wrote underneath: *Contact not reachable directly. Program director's office abstaining from comment.*

It was Dmytro who said it.

They sat on Wednesday evening in the mess hall after dinner. She and Petro were at the far table reviewing extraction parameters for the next interval. Marta was making tea. Oleh had his tablet. Dmytro came in from his exercises, filled a glass from the filter jug at the counter, and said without turning around:

“Turn off the uplink for the next extraction.”

Petro’s pen stopped.

Dmytro turned. He held the glass in both hands – the grip of a man whose left hand didn’t close all the way anymore.

“There is someone in the signal,” he said. “Like when they jam the signal and GPS says you’re in Peru. Take away the signal. See what you get.”

He said it in a flat voice, already certain, like he had said sulfur a week earlier.

Marta’s kettle clicked off.

“We do it on Saturday,” Hanna said. “Andrii, could you disconnect the uplink before the drilling?”

Andrii nodded once. Dmytro finished his water and left. She heard his counting resume a few minutes later.

On Saturday, Andrii disconnected the satellite uplink. The instruments ran on local power and local processing anyway. The satellite connection was for transmission, not operation.

The drill ran. The core came up.

The core showed standard sediment with some mineral content and trace particles. She found no ancient bacteria, no diatoms, no sulfur. She'd been pulling cores like this since they started – unremarkable, consistent with the geological profile, worth logging and forgetting. Manual cross-checks confirmed what the sensors showed. The hardware she'd been documenting since the start of the rotation read clean.

She ran her protocols. Everything was ordinary.

Andrii restored the uplink at 14:00. Emails queued and sent. Weather data synced.

Tuesday came. They ran the next extraction with the internet restored and all systems running normally.

The results were ordinary. Sediment, mineral traces, nothing worth a second look.

She ran the protocols anyway. Standing in the station lab at midnight, checking the same surfaces she'd checked that morning, writing down the same zeros. Outside, the wind had dropped. The silence that followed was the kind only Antarctica produced – no traffic, no machinery, no voices, just ice settling under its own weight and the sea moving against the shore in the dark.

The anomaly was gone. It came through the signal, probably, from outside the station. It was not her people.

Weeks after the anomaly stopped, Petro told her he'd used his Thursday satellite phone slot to call Nik in Warsaw, a glaciologist he'd studied with years ago and stayed in contact with ever since.

He'd told him everything. Framed it carefully, hedged – probably nothing, equipment maybe. But strange enough that he wanted someone outside the station to know.

Nik, she thought. *Mykola, who had decided to become Polish.*

She'd already seen the Warsaw number in the satellite log before he mentioned it.

She nodded. The information would spread regardless.

Tomás found it weeks later – an automated search alert had flagged a topic on a glaciologist's forum. Someone at Vernadsky had told a colleague, who'd mentioned it in an email, who'd posted it. Most of the replies were jokes about cabin fever. He read past those; he was used to such comments about his own observations.

What was crucial was that the anomaly existed only with an internet connection, and it matched other unexplained observations in his notebook.

He emailed one of his acquaintances, a geologist working in Greenland, and asked if it was possible to find diatoms and sulfur during low-depth Antarctic drilling. The answer was vague – it was barely possible, and if confirmed, it would be a tremendous scientific event. But he had heard nothing of the sort. And the topic on the forum he referred to might just be a joke.

He added Vernadsky to the file anyway.

CHAPTER 16

The Bait

An email arrived the next morning. From the Belém source – the Gentleman, as she'd come to call him. A single line: *FYI. This came to me through a contact I trust. Handle with care.*

The attachment loaded slowly.

Internal Communications – Meridian Project, Phase I – II.

She fed it to the inkjet. The printer coughed and started printing. She stood at the counter while it worked. The cartridge was running low, the ink thinning at the margins.

Budget authorizations across three participating agencies. A development timeline with code names she recognized from Alameda files. A technical architecture section. And coordinates for the primary research node – a facility in northern Finland.

The Finnish coordinates. She had seen them before. The satellite imagery from the university archive had shown a facility at those coordinates in 2027, and an empty forest where it had been by 2029.

She carried the pages to Tomás. "The Belém source just sent us something."

He worked through the document, turning pages, going back, turning forward again. Maren watched his face.

He was on page six, the technical architecture section, and he'd slowed down. He went back two pages. Read something again.

She waited.

"When did this arrive?"

"This morning. He says it came from a contact he trusts." She paused. "The Finnish coordinates match the satellite imagery. Two independent sources pointing at the same facility. This is publishable, Tomás."

He was on page eight. His hand had stopped moving. He read the same part three times.

"It's wrong."

"What do you mean, wrong?"

"The architecture. This describes a centralized system – hub-and-spoke, a single primary node in Finland." He picked up the page. "Meridian was distributed. The Auriga logs showed it running from different addresses across four continents shortly after launch. No hub. No single point of failure."

She looked at the Finnish coordinates again. A real site. A real facility. But the wrong architecture for the system it claimed to describe. "Someone built this to be believed," she said. "And aimed at us."

Her mug was in her hand. She turned it in her fingers. The Gentleman had sent her a document pointing to a site she'd already found. That was how you made disinformation irresistible – you confirmed what the target already believed.

Then she looked at Tomás. "How do you know what the distribution framework looks like?"

"That's how I designed it – so it couldn't be taken down from one location."

"You designed?"

"Yes, in Delft."

She stayed silent for several long seconds.

"Tomás. What else haven't you told me?"

He sat down. The flat voice he used for technical summaries. "Eight years ago I worked on a project in Delft Technical University. Elena Ross was its supervisor. I built the tools. The distribution framework, the optimization logic, the failover architecture." He spread his arms. "When I saw the logs, I recognized my own work. Extended, deployed at a scale I never intended."

"You've known since the Auriga server."

"Yes."

"That was days ago. We've been sitting here, working on this together, and you knew that the thing we're investigating runs on code you wrote."

"I was afraid you'd think I was part of it. That I knew what it would become."

"Did you?"

"No. I built disaster response tools. They turned it into something else after I left." He looked at her. "I don't know where the line is between what I built and what it became."

There was a self-service laundromat on the next block – automated, AI-powered, touchless. Someone had put a brick through its front window, and a sticker on the door read NO AI. They had found another one two streets over – coin-operated, no attendant, a row of machines from the previous decade. The door didn't lock properly and swung open when the machines shifted cycles. They went early, before the neighborhood woke, and sat on the plastic chairs while the drum turned. The air smelled of detergent and warm lint. Maren combed her hair with her fingers, still damp from the shower. Neither of them spoke. The machine hummed. It was the most ordinary hour they'd had in a week.

On the walk back, a long-haul truck sat parked across the entrance of an automated warehouse, a hand-painted banner over it: *PEOPLE OVER MACHINES*. The Terra Livre cable attacks were on every screen now – cafés, kiosks, the pharmacy waiting area. They had claimed a datacenter outside Frankfurt the night before. The group had not existed three months ago.

That afternoon she called Marcus Cole. His SEC filing was public record – she'd found it in a list of hearings related to Harwell-Kirk. A quantitative analyst from New York, who had flagged Harwell-Kirk Capital's spending shift and had been fired for it. He reported to the SEC, but then withdrew his claim, citing a conflict of interest.

She tracked him through a professional network and called from the prepaid line.

He answered after a few rings. He sounded like a man who had been waiting for this call for a long time.

"We have been funding university research for years," he said. "Normal grants, nothing unusual. Then around 2026, everything changed. The money stopped going to universities and started going into our own facilities – in Finland, Brazil, Southeast Asia. The subsidiaries were completely opaque and built from scratch. They had bought server hardware and hired all kinds of engineers, as if they were building research centers for someone. All while Harwell-Kirk Capital was listed as a real estate operator, occasionally sponsoring environmental research." He paused. "I flagged it as a possible money laundering issue. They gave me two weeks' notice. And…"

His voice became lower. “When I tried to prove I was just doing my work, things got weird. Six-figure weird. So I agreed to withdraw my claim. That ended my career. I retired.”

Maren tried to choose her words carefully. “Was it negotiated, or pushed?”

“They hinted at potential problems, but I won’t be giving you any details. Sorry.”

“I understand. Is there anything else? Have you found what they were researching?”

“Well, yes,” he said, hesitating. “Within a year, all the centers were closed down. They stopped whatever they were doing in the facilities and redirected the money somewhere else – a technology company. Noctis Labs.”

She knew the name. Everyone did. Noctis Labs had been the fastest-growing tech company in Europe that year – Forbes had run a cover story on them. They made Scribe, the AI writing platform that half the world used.

“Mr. Cole, I know what this costs you. Thank you.”

“Just don’t use my name.”

“I won’t.”

He wished her luck, and they hung up.

She told Tomás. “There is no way anyone could create something like Scribe in a year,” he said. “Regardless of their money.”

“Then how? Did they buy it from a third party?”

“Then we would have known about it. I think they took their own previous project and built on it.”

“Meridian.”

“Most likely. With safeguards to avoid escape.”

She recalled that Dietrich from Berlin had mentioned her Noctis Labs once – a story he'd been working on, something about corporate ownership that had gone nowhere. She'd paid no attention at the time. She called him on an online messenger.

"Dietrich. I'm sorry I never wrote back."

"Maren." A pause. "Where the hell have you been?"

"Working, investigating off the record." She steadied her voice. "What do you know about Noctis Labs?"

"I tried investigating them six months ago," he said. "My editor killed the story before I had a draft. The Consortium told me they wouldn't publish anything Scribe-related. The ownership is layered – a New York fund, private investors, a few tech giants. Nobody wants their name on it, and nobody has to." He exhaled. "The only name I could pin to anything was on the patent filings. Dr. Elena Ross. Does that mean anything to you?"

"It does."

"Then you know more than I do." He paused. "Maren, stay away from Noctis. Half the parliament uses Scribe. Ministers, commissioners. Anyone who goes after that company will find a lot of very powerful people standing in the way."

"Thank you, Dietrich. I mean it."

"Write back this time," he said, and hung up.

That evening, Maren asked Tomás if he had a way to reach Ross. He did – an old university address from the Delft days, buried in a backup he'd carried in the notebook. He typed the message on the secondhand laptop while she watched.

Dr. Ross, this is Tomás Herrera. We worked together at TU Delft. I need to ask you about Meridian. Please reply.

He sent it. No reply came.

The next morning, her phone rang at 6:47. Not her private number – the prepaid SIM's own number, the one she'd bought for cash and never given to anyone. The only call she had made from it was to Cole a day before.

She answered.

"Maren, my dear." The voice from the Belém café. The same courtesy, the same considered pauses. "I do apologize for the hour. I sent you that document hoping you would use it. I see that you did not."

She said nothing.

"I gave you a name, and the name was the story. You had one simple task – show the world what Meridian is, why it should be stopped. Instead, you chose to investigate the people who are trying to stop it." A pause. "You might also ask Mr. Herrera about his work on distributed systems, though I suspect you've already had that conversation."

His voice didn't change for what came next.

"His daughter attends the Escola Santa Maria, fifth year, Mrs. Oliveira's class. Lovely school – jacaranda trees in the courtyard, if I remember correctly. I would like you to share those details with your partner, and I would like both of you to consider very carefully what you do next."

The line clicked dead.

Maren placed the phone on the table with both hands.

She turned and saw Tomás in the doorway. He might have heard something or seen it on her face.

"What?"

"Escola Santa Maria. Fifth year. Mrs. Oliveira's class," she said, her voice crackling. "Jacaranda trees in the courtyard."

His jaw worked. “We have to stop. Whatever we have, wherever it is, it isn’t worth it.”

She inhaled.

“They won’t touch her,” she said. “She’s leverage. She only works as leverage if she’s safe.”

“I’m not going to take this risk. The photo was a hint. We pursued it, and now there is a threat.”

“Tomás, they are not omnipresent. It’s not a secret cabal, killing people and destroying lives – they are a technology company with a private security arm. They could erase your documents, but they don’t know about the farm and won’t go there for her.”

“How can you be sure? You have nothing to lose, but I can’t risk her!”

“They have my brother.”

“And you are willing to risk his life? For your investigation?”

“It’s not only about the investigation,” she said. “Those people have created a system that is self-replicating and lives somewhere on the internet. And then they created another one and installed it on every lawmaker’s device in the world.”

Then she continued, “And it was *you* who made it decentralized and self-replicating. I need *you* for this.”

CHAPTER 17

Every Door

The apartment was starting to gnaw at Maren.

It was the same place it had been for two weeks – the two mattresses, the folding table, the gas stove, the pull-cord light. The printer sat on the kitchen counter, its paper tray not quite flush. The ink ran out, and Tomás had to refill it with a syringe twice – a replacement cartridge cost twice as much as they paid for the printer. The flat smelled of ink and cardboard.

Maren sat with her laptop at one end of the table. Tomás worked at the other. They ate at different times, rinsed their cups separately, and said what needed saying and not much else.

Tomás's *we have to stop* was still in the room with them. She didn't disagree with it, not exactly, but she pushed, and he folded.

The investigation was not finished, but at least there was a part of it worth publishing: Scribe was built on technologies from the university projects.

She'd tried her channels first. The European Investigative Consortium – the cross-border journalist network Maren had used for the lobbying series – had bounced for days. The domain returned a registrar parking page. She tried the cached version through the Wayback Machine and got a snapshot from three weeks earlier. The contact form behind it went nowhere.

Henrik, her editor at Berlingske, went to a mailbox that no longer accepted messages. The intelligence source on the protected messenger had been dark since her state actors article.

Étienne had sent an unencrypted email directly to her – his outreach had probably already been logged somewhere, which made him a liability now, not a channel. Every door that had been open in the first weeks of this was closed.

"If Ross created Scribe as Plan B – what was its purpose?" she said. "Fight Meridian, or just earn money?"

Tomás looked up from his notebook. "If two autonomous systems were fighting on the internet, there would be visible disruption. Escalating automated attacks, infrastructure shutting down." He shook his head. "I see nothing like that."

At least what they had was publishable. The corporate trail from Harwell-Kirk through the construction facilities to Noctis Labs, and the theory that Scribe was built on Meridian's codebase. It was enough to force regulatory scrutiny – if it reached the right person.

"Do you know Manuela Mendes?" she asked.

Tomás nodded. "The investigative channel. Two million subscribers."

"Dietrich introduced us last year, when he was still working on the Noctis story. She's been covering financial fraud in Southern Europe for eight years – off-book accounts, shell companies, revenue authority corruption. No institutional leash. No newspaper lawyer, no parent company with a board to call." Maren pulled up the channel on her laptop. The latest video was posted four days ago: forty-three minutes on the Iberian revenue authority, broadcast-quality audio. "She's based in London."

"Every person we contact gets targeted," Tomás said. "Nuno, for instance."

"You don't know that," she said. "He might have gone to see his uncle in Macau."

"Or he was erased, as they tried to do to me. And now you want to contact someone else."

"She's in London, Tomás. Not Portugal. Different jurisdiction, different police, different courts. They can't send PJ officers to raid a flat in Hackney."

"Why don't we publish it ourselves? We don't need a journalist – we'll put it somewhere it can't be taken down."

"A document nobody reads." She shrugged. "Mendes has two million subscribers and the infrastructure to publish before anyone gets an injunction. I don't even have an Instagram page."

"How do you contact her?"

"I have a secure channel through Dietrich. She already knows my name."

"You're assuming she won't be afraid to go after Scribe."

"I'm assuming it's the best option we have left."

He didn't agree, but he never stopped her.

Maren assembled the package that evening. The corporate funding trail – Harwell-Kirk Capital through private facilities to Noctis Labs. The theory that Scribe was built on Meridian's codebase. Cole's testimony, anonymized. Her protest amplification data and the 14ms bot signature that matched Meridian's design. Two halves of a story she couldn't yet connect. She stripped her own metadata, wrote a cover note laying out what she had and what she didn't, and encrypted the archive with Mendes's public key from Dietrich.

She sent it to the secure email. The upload bar crawled across the screen and finished.

In the middle of the night, turning and unable to sleep, she typed a message to Kasper's number – the one that had gone to voicemail three times since she left Copenhagen.

She wrote it in Danish. She told him that the posts he'd been sharing had been amplified by a bot network. That the protests he'd joined were being coordinated by automated systems she couldn't yet identify. She didn't tell him about Meridian or Ross or the investigation. She told him what she could prove: his social network activity had been identified, targeted, and boosted. Someone had aimed his anger and timed the amplification to when he was most active.

The reply came at 3 a.m. One line: *You have chosen your side. Don't write me anymore.*

He was twenty-four. He was an adult. She couldn't pull him out of this – he was not brainwashed, not in a cult. That was a logical evolution of his rebellious nature. Even if it was against progress.

They spent half of the next day packing the bags, printing the documents, and tearing the drafts into small pieces.

Tomás found it on the news aggregator.

Mendes's channel had been removed. *Content violation under emergency digital safety protocols.* Her flat in London had been raided by the Metropolitan Police and Europol. Alleged tax evasion – a charge that needed no evidence to file and took a minimum of eight months to dismiss. Equipment confiscated. Mendes herself detained for processing, released pending investigation.

London. Different jurisdiction, different police, different courts. Twelve hours.

Tomás said, “You did this.”

“I know.”

“Nuno. Now Mendes.”

“I know, Tomás.”

“People are not tools.” His voice was louder than she’d heard it. He was standing now. “You don’t get to use them and then say you know. Nuno is gone. Mendes has a daughter, and you sent her a message, and twelve hours later men were at her door.”

“It’s bigger than–”

He was looking at her. “You can’t pretend you don’t care about them and then keep asking them to risk everything.”

He was right, and she couldn’t say it.

The courtyard was quiet. A motorcycle went through the entrance too fast and startled the pigeons.

She stood at the table for a long time. He sat back down. The screen had refreshed, the channel URL redirecting to an error message.

“I…” Her voice croaked. “I wanted – I want you to know that I *do* care, Tomás.”

He looked at her. “But?”

“No buts.”

He sat quietly for a minute, then nodded.

The knocking came at 1:40 AM.

“*Polícia. Verificação de segurança.*”

Tomás moved to the door, putting on his pants and taking out his driver’s license. Maren grabbed her coat, but he motioned her to stay back, out of the entryway. A foreign woman, not speaking Portuguese, in a rental apartment at two in the morning, might complicate things.

She reached for her coat and took out the pepper spray and showed it to him. He shook his head and she hid it, but still held her coat close.

He opened the door partway.

Two officers: one in his forties, the other younger, a detail card in his hand. The older one had shaving irritation along his jaw. The older one's flashlight searched the apartment through the opening, then moved to Tomás's face. He held his other hand close to the belt.

"There has been a report of suspicious activity in the building. How many persons are inside? Your identification?"

Tomás answered the questions politely and handed over his driver's license. The older one looked at it, turned it to the photo, looked at Tomás and checked his personal terminal, then handed the license back.

If his name was flagged somewhere in the federal system, the officer's terminal either hadn't synced, was offline, or was one of the things that had stopped working.

Maren stepped forward enough to be visible. The Danish passport was in her coat pocket. She held it out.

The older officer took it, examined it, and handed it back without checking on the terminal.

"*Obrigado.*" He glanced once more into the apartment. "*Boa noite.*"

Tomás closed the apartment door and looked at Maren.

"Coincidence?" he asked.

She shrugged. "Not sure it was about suspicious activity."

"It wasn't." He locked the door. "An anonymous report tonight, of all nights? Somebody put us on the list. This was a warning."

“We should move soon.”

“Where?”

“Denmark. I have options there.” She reached over and took his hand.

He let her.

CHAPTER 18
The Testimony

The gas stove sat on the counter where it always sat – blue metal, single burner, the butane canister attached. It took two strikes to catch. Maren held the lighter with her thumb, watching the gas tick through two clicks before the ring went blue, then turned it down until the flame was barely there. She'd been working the stove carefully since the Copenhagen call – the gas valve, the kettle handle, the mug she set on the counter.

Tomás sat at the table with a second-hand laptop open, his elbows on the table, reading something. His notebook and pen rested by his side.

Her own laptop had many fewer tabs and documents open than usual – there was not much to do now. She'd opened the Kasper folder in the morning and hadn't closed it. Green jacket, 2029, Christiansborg. His chin up, hands in his pockets.

The windowsill where pigeons usually landed was bare.

She poured the water into two mugs. Put a tea bag in one, then reached for the instant coffee and stopped. She smiled to herself and put a tea bag in her mug too.

She brought Tomás his mug and stood by his side for a moment.

"I need to show you something."

She pulled her laptop around and turned it to face him. She tapped the trackpad, waking it, and the photograph came back: Kasper in the green jacket she'd bought him for his twentieth birthday.

Tomás looked at the screen.

"He's my brother," she said. "Kasper. He's twenty-four."

She continued, "Our parents split when he was nine. When I went to university, he came to live with me in Copenhagen – not officially. Father was in Odense, our mother spent most of her time in her garden and couldn't control a fifteen-year-old. I drove him to school. Helped with applications. Covered for him past curfew." She paused. "He used to eat cereal dry out of the box while reading conspiracy forums on his phone. I bought him that jacket for his twentieth birthday. It was too big in the shoulders that year. In the photo, he's at the purist protest in Copenhagen."

"Have you been in contact with him lately?"

"Not exactly. He texted me the day I found the synchronization data: *Can we talk?* I was not ready for it. I was going to call him that night, but never did. I texted and tried to call him for three weeks, but he'd stopped answering." She paused. "Last night I sent him a message. I told him his posts had been amplified by a bot network. That someone was targeting his activity and timing the recruitment windows." She looked at the photograph. "He wrote back at three in the morning, saying that we're now on opposite sides."

Tomás had set his tea down.

"He's been active on purist forums since at least mid-2028. I identified his handle in the amplification data after I came to Lisbon." She pointed at the screen – not at Kasper's face, but at the document with his posts and thousands of reactions under them. "The bot cluster pushed his posts to the top of every feed. He was in the target profile."

A police siren outside made them both glance at the window. It slowly faded, and they turned back to her laptop.

"He wasn't only at the Christiansborg march – he was in Frankfurt too. And maybe at others, helping, organizing, igniting." She tapped the trackpad. The photo gallery of the green jacket filled half the screen. "They don't just have his data. They're using him to coordinate the protests."

She closed the photos.

"That's the name I didn't tell you."

Then she opened a second tab – the amplification data from October, the social activity timestamps.

"Someone had identified his anger and aimed it." She let him look at the data. "The system we're investigating weaponized my brother. The system you helped build."

Tomás looked at the data for a long time.

"I worked on a disaster response system," he said. "Not a weapon."

"But it became one."

"Not exactly. The one I built was decentralized – this one is different."

"You hid that from me anyway."

"You hid the surveillance, and that your brother was helping coordinate the protests."

"That's not the same–"

"You knew you were being watched before we even met." He turned a page in the notebook, going nowhere. "You contacted Mendes when I said not to. You pushed me to stay when I wanted to leave." He turned another page. "I hid my involvement. You hid men with guns."

"You were already under surveillance in Brazil," she said. "Your mother was visited. Your drives were taken. You called me, Tomás. You said you were coming."

"I called you because I thought you were safe." His voice was quiet. "I didn't know I was running toward the same thing I was running from. Mendes has a daughter. Did you know that?"

"I did." She wrapped both hands around her mug. "Mendes is a journalist. Risk is part of her job."

"Her daughter is not part of the *job*. Neither is mine."

She set her mug back on the table. "We both kept things back. We both had reasons for it." She paused. "So what do we do now?"

Tomás looked at the photograph on her screen.

"We need to write it down," he said. "All of it. Everything we found, related or not."

She took her laptop and moved to the opposite side of the table.

She started with the synchronization data. Two months of it – twenty-two outages across fifteen countries, hundreds of bot-cluster activations. And the fourteen-millisecond spike she'd first calculated at the Berlingske desk. By now there were hundreds of protests worldwide; she didn't try to track them anymore. A quick check had shown that the outages and amplifications were still there.

She documented the push of purist accounts with the bot farm. The social activity mapped to protest dates, the anger-to-action pipeline that turned online posting into street presence. She wrote the handle as an example: *nordisk_ansen*, and lingered on it for a while. Then the journalist won, and she wrote: *His name is Kasper Eliasson, 24, my brother*. She documented the social networks' activity dates, increased posting frequency in the weeks before the

Frankfurt protests, where she found him. The last recorded activity was three days before the Christiansborg march.

She included the Meridian project. Professor Almeida's boxes in the university basement. The photograph, the architecture diagrams, the 14ms letter that connected the project's design to the bot-network signature. The Meridian roster with twelve entities obtained from the university network. The Auriga Trading relay logs that showed the system being tested on live markets, and the subject line that said it had escaped.

She documented Harwell-Kirk Capital and its funding strategies. The capital shift that Cole had flagged when the money moved from universities to construction facilities and then to Noctis Labs. Noctis was only an operator for Scribe, not a developer. She wrote their theory that Scribe was based on a Meridian codebase, with safeguards, and packaged as a personal assistant. She did not know what connected it to the protests.

She noted that content from someone surveilling her and Tomás had leaked into a writer's Scribe folder.

She documented what had been done to stop the investigation. The Copenhagen apartment fire. The Graça flat break-in with her brother's birthday on a slip of paper. The threats, the false leads. The source who had threatened a child when they went off-script.

She mentioned people who had helped or hindered them: Henrik, Nuno, Lacroix, Dietrich, Mendes, Schmitt, Cole, and the Gentleman – she had never learned his real name or position.

Tomás opened a fresh document on the second-hand laptop and started typing. His notebook was open beside him, and he transcribed from it – dates in the margin where he had them, approximate dates where he didn't. He had been keeping this log in his head and on paper since before he left São Paulo. Now he put it down in electronic form.

He started with anomalies that were likely his paranoia or surveillance. The traffic light. The bike with a dent, his data taken during the blackout, when nothing had worked. Lúcia's tablet, reacting to barking. The stranger in his mother's care home who pretended he couldn't recognize her. Then he listed unexplainable events that could have been just him seeing patterns. The lime vendor. The unexplainable results from the drills at the Antarctic station.

He wrote the incidents in order. He gave each one a probable cause where he had one. Where the probable cause held, he wrote it plainly. Where it didn't, he left the cell empty.

Then he moved on to his life being erased, his passport stolen, and his credit cards blocked.

Then his mother's conversation with the men who had walked into her care home room, past reception, past staff.

Laithe & Bonn. The office that existed one day and was removed the next, the scratches still visible on the floor.

The beating in the garage.

The threats to Lúcia.

The technical work he did for Maren. Analyzing the bot's 14 ms delay. Data analysis. The phone IMEI change. The laptop hacking. The Auriga server tracing and exploiting. It was the only part resembling his work as an engineer.

Dr. Elena Ross. The project at TU Delft she led, the disaster response toolset, the distributed failsafe system. Months of work before the funding changed and the NDAs came. What he'd seen in the Auriga relay log – her address in the headers. His work in the logs. Then: *I did not tell M. E. about this.*

He looked at what he had. Some were anomalies. Some were events with correlations to Maren's data. Some were internet rumors. And half of the document was devoted to the investigation in Lisbon, where he withheld information, was beaten, and stayed passive, letting Maren lead. After two decades of working with software, after designing a system that was able to replicate itself on the internet, he was now reduced to a jumpy man with a Moleskine.

And he regretted nothing.

She read his section while he read hers.

The light through the kitchen window had gone from white to ochre. A television somewhere in the building next door was too loud.

She stopped at the anomaly log. The lime vendor. The Vernadsky forum thread. The column that held probable causes was empty for half the entries.

"This part," she said, scrolling through the unexplainable section on his laptop. "This undermines the credibility of everything before it."

He was reading her financial section on her screen.

"We have satellite imagery, financial records, and latency analysis," she continued. "Any investigator who gets to a column of blanks will stop reading."

"I know." He looked at her screen one more time. "If we're writing the truth, it's all of it."

They left it in.

They cleared the table. Tomás went to the closet and came back with a roll of tape, a marker, and two pizza boxes that still smelled of cheese. They tore the boxes flat and taped them to the wall above the table. Maren started writing on sticky notes and drawing lines on the cardboard.

She wrote each name, each connection, each date on a separate note and stuck it to the cardboard. Tomás added his entries from the laptop, scrolling through the document as he went. They worked for two hours.

When they stepped back, the wall looked like a conspiracy theorist's bedroom. And, strictly speaking, it was. Sticky notes in clusters. Lines drawn in marker between them. Dates. Arrows.

Maren stepped back from the board. The protest cluster on the right held outages, the amplification data, Kasper, Schmitt, Kessler, IASO, the beating, Mendes, the break-ins. The Meridian cluster in the middle – Almeida, roster, Auriga, the escape. Harwell-Kirk on the left – properties, Cole, Noctis Labs, Scribe. The Gentleman in the corner with an arrow pointing at Meridian and the word STEER.

She took the marker and drew a big circle with a question mark above the protest cluster.

"Who is behind them?" she said. "Why? What's the motive?"

The only weak link they had between Harwell-Kirk's side and the protest side was L&B on Kessler's old client list. It didn't name anyone.

"Start with what we know," Tomás said. "Ross developed Meridian across universities. It escaped through Auriga. She wrote Plan B. Then Harwell-Kirk moved the money into private facilities, built Scribe, and demolished the labs."

"But that doesn't explain the secrecy," Maren said. "The demolitions, Cole being silenced – none of that fits a commercial product."

"So what is it for?"

The television next door was still too loud. Neither of them moved to close the window.

“And there’s still the fourteen milliseconds,” Maren said quietly. “The bots carry the same signature as Meridian’s design, the same timer precision from Almeida’s email.”

Tomás looked at the board, then at her.

“Maren. Can you pull when Scribe first entered different markets?”

She opened the laptop. Noctis had filed with national regulators before each market launch – stock disclosures, estimated valuations, launch dates. She searched the European filings. Germany had been first, in March. France in May. Britain and Ireland in the summer. Spain and Portugal by November. The Nordics by December.

She printed the page.

Tomás took the printout and carried it to the board. He pinned it next to the protest timeline – the dates she had charted months ago, the bot cluster activations country by country.

Germany: Scribe had launched in March, and the first bot activations came in late April. France followed the same pattern – May, then June. Spain, Portugal, Sweden all showed the same gap. Five to seven weeks after each market entry, the first coordinated amplification appeared.

“Scribe is the bot factory,” he said. “Every device running Scribe is a node. When a region reaches thousands of installations, their owners got enough to generate localized protests at scale.” He put his finger on the question mark she’d drawn. “Ross didn’t abandon the fight. She built a weapon and got it installed on millions of devices. She’s not waging an internet war against Meridian – she’s turning the physical world against the AI.”

PART 4: THE SILENCE

CHAPTER 19

The Last Morning

The electricity cut off sometime before dawn. Tomás woke to the beeping of power supplies throughout the building.

Grey light came through the courtyard windows. The pull-cord light was dead. The laptops still had charge but were useless without a network. The big makeshift whiteboard hung above the table beside the printed pages, still squared where Maren had stacked them. Tomás had fallen asleep in his clothes – he hadn't bothered to change after they finished writing. His neck ached on the left side. His ribs protested when he moved.

Maren was at the table. She'd been awake longer, re-reading the testimony. The two printed copies lay stacked on the table: forty-two pages each.

The drives were hidden, the testimony printed, the whiteboard photographed and printed, and the bags stood by the door.

He got up. He took the igniter and turned the valve on the gas canister for the stove. The flame came up blue. He held his palm above it for a second.

There were four eggs left in the paper carton on the counter and a third of a loaf of bread. He cracked the first egg one-handed against the rim of the pan, pulled the shell apart, and it came clean. He shook the pan in slow circles and kept the heat low. The whites set before the yolks did. Two eggs in the pan, then two more. He didn't have a second burner, so he held a slice of bread against the pan's side by hand and turned it when it started to char. Steam rose, and the fat from the eggs popped once against his wrist. He pulled his hand back, not quite burned. He put a kettle on the fire and, when it whistled, dropped tea bags into the mugs.

He caught Maren's gaze. She was smiling at him.

He cleared the table, wiped it with a dish towel, set two plates – hers had a blue band around the rim; his was plain white – and divided the eggs between them, putting the toast on the side.

Maren sat down. He watched her eat, then started eating too, because there was nothing else to do.

The tea was bitter, but the eggs were good.

Through the window, the street was empty. No movement, just the shuttered pharmacy and the still air.

Maren picked up her mug.

"Let me guess," she said. "Lúcia's a difficult customer."

"She is." He moved the fork to the edge of his plate. "What gives it away? The eggs or the toast?"

"The eggs."

"She wanted them hard for about a year. Said runny was disgusting. Then she came home from a friend's house and decided she'd been wrong." He shrugged. "It took another six months before she'd admit it to me."

Maren laughed. He looked at her, and he was laughing too.

She set down her mug. The plates were mostly empty.

He washed them under the cold tap – no hot water without power – and stacked them on the counter to dry. Through the window, the street looked different. No vendors setting up. The pharmacy across the road had its shutters down, and someone had taped a handwritten note to the glass that he could not read from this distance. An autonomous taxi sat motionless on the road, unable to connect to a dispatch server. On the far side, a woman on a third-floor balcony was hanging laundry on a drying rack, working through a basket of wet clothes as if the morning was ordinary.

He thought about Lúcia. He could not call her from a prepaid line – it had no international coverage. The cell signal was carrying voice but not data, and the satellite relay needed data to connect. There was no way to reach Diamantina from this kitchen. He didn't know if the farm had power. He didn't know if Carolina had fuel. He stood at the sink with the water still running and let himself not know for a moment, then he turned the tap off and dried his hands.

He repacked the bags. Everything they needed was already in them.

Half an hour later, Maren reached for her phone. "I need to try it once more."

The signal was patchy but working – the European networks were stripped down to voice, but not dead.

She called Henrik.

He answered on the second ring. She heard the background noise – the newsroom was still functioning. "Maren, where the hell are you? The world is coming apart – capitals going black one by one, military on the streets!"

"I have a story. The real one. Sourced, documented. About purists and protests."

A pause. She could hear him breathing.

"Maren, we can't run it." His voice was flat, final. "The board won't allow anything about infrastructure right now – emergency press protocols."

Then his voice dropped to almost nothing.

"The only story they'll accept from you is about some crazy AI. Those were the exact words. I don't know what it means, but I have to follow them."

She tried two more outlets. A fellow data journalist in Amsterdam was in crisis mode, dealing with rolling blackouts. A Brussels contact at an NGO went to voicemail – full.

Then her phone buzzed with a hidden number on the prepaid line.

"Ms. Eliasson." She recognized Schmitt's voice. It wasn't polished anymore. Tired, cracking. "We are shutting down operations. The situation has exceeded our capacity to manage." A pause. "You need to leave Lisbon. I can't halt the outstanding orders."

"Wait, what about–"

The line went dead.

She stood at the window. She could see smoke south of the river – two columns rising over the far bank. Military trucks were moving south on the Ponte 25 de Abril. From a block away, she heard the loudspeaker before she saw the car – a recorded voice echoing off the buildings. The car turned the corner and crawled up their street.

Tomás translated for her: "They are asking people to stay indoors. A curfew will be enacted at night."

She turned to him.

"Schmitt called. Said they are out of business – protests got out of control. But he told us to leave anyway." She chewed her lip. "I will try to reach Denmark and stay in the cabin I told you about. Are you with me?"

She held her breath.

He gave her a warm smile. "I'm with you."

CHAPTER 20
Cascade

They walked to Santa Apolónia because the metro was down.

Down the stairwell first – they passed the cracked tile on the landing between second and third, the elevator with its out-of-order sign that had been there since October. Someone had left a plastic bag of tangerines by the mailboxes. Then the building door, and the street.

They walked twenty minutes down Almirante Reis, the main artery of Arroios. The street was quiet. A café on the corner was open, its radio running on batteries. It was repeating an emergency broadcast, and the barista was wiping down the counter with a cloth, working the same six-inch stretch of laminate. The cart vendors on Almirante Reis weren't there. A man in a ground-floor apartment was taping a window from the inside, strips of brown packing tape in a grid pattern.

Farther down the avenue, closer to Intendente, military trucks moved in convoy. Green and canvas-sided, they rolled slowly. Young soldiers sat in the beds, staring out at the city, rifles braced upright between their knees. One of them was eating something from a wrapper. She counted eight. Civilians stayed inside, their electric cars out of charge. Lisbon had banned gas cars in the centre a long time ago, built an infrastructure for EVs, and now all of it was dead.

The train to Porto smelled of cleaning fluid and old diesel exhaust, the latter from the boxy locomotive CP had hitched to the front when the catenary went dead. The carriage was packed, with people standing in the vestibule. Out the window, the Tagus widened; the ochre rooflines of the suburbs gave way to open fields. Cristo Rei stood on the south bank with its arms spread. She looked at it for a moment, then the curve of the track carried the statue out of sight. A woman across the aisle was knitting a blue scarf or a sweater – Maren couldn't tell.

On the platform in Santa Iria, she saw a man in a dark blazer standing still in the moving crowd. For a second she thought of Schmitt. Then the crowd shifted, and the man was gone. On their last call he had said, *We are shutting down operations.* Did that mean they were off the hook, or just that nobody was left to give the orders?

The train died in Coimbra.

There was no announcement. The lights flickered, then the diesel engine sound dropped. The carriage coasted on momentum; the deceleration was so gradual that the stop came before she registered it. They almost made it to the station.

Nobody moved for a full minute. A child two rows up said something to its mother. The mother said, "Shh."

The conductor ran by, saying that the engine needed maintenance and they would be on the move shortly, in an hour or two maximum. Nobody believed her.

They got their bags and filed out onto the track, then walked to the platform. A railway worker in a reflective vest was standing by the signal box, smoking. Maren asked him how to find a car. He looked at them for a second and then told them the center had banned ICE for years, which meant no fuel stations inside the ring. They'd have to walk to the outskirts. Every petrol station still open out there had a few old diesel or petrol cars in the lot – farmers started offloading them for cash, asking three times the worth. He pointed them to a paper map on the wall inside the station. They took one.

They walked into Coimbra. The streets were old stone and cobblestone, and the university sat on the hill above them. A pharmacy two blocks from the station had a queue out the door – people were standing outside, chatting loudly and complaining that they were operating on cash only. Students sat on the steps of a church with dead phones in their laps. A café on the corner had dragged a camping stove onto the sidewalk and was selling espresso from a moka pot, one cup at a time, the line moving slowly, the smell of coffee cutting through the street. An autonomous delivery robot sat at the curb with its lid open and its cargo compartment empty, the routing screen dark.

They walked east through the old town toward the outer ring, past shuttered shops and a bookstore with a handwritten sign in the window: *Aberto. Temos velas – *Open. We have candles.

The man at the petrol station outside Coimbra drove a hard bargain for thirty seconds and then agreed to cash, no paperwork, keys handed over in a petrol-stained palm. Tomás handled it – Portuguese, fast and flat, just settling it. The car was a Renault Clio, ten years old, with a manual transmission and 180,000 kilometers on the dash. It also had a crack in the windshield that ran from the passenger corner halfway across, held at the end with a strip of clear tape that was yellowing. Tomás put their bags in the back and got in the passenger seat. The pine air freshener hanging from the mirror had stopped smelling like pine some time ago. The gearshift was making a grinding sound between second and third when she tested it in the car park. She told him; he nodded and said they were out of options anyway.

They took the A25 east. The border at Vilar Formoso was unmanned, the booth empty and the barrier up. They drove under it without slowing.

They crossed into Spain, and the landscape changed within twenty miles – the Castilian meseta opening out under a flat winter sky with no clouds and too much grey light.

The radio was cycling between news and government advisories in Spanish. They caught the basic phrases – nuclear stations down, infrastructure disruptions, military deployments. Citizens were advised to limit non-essential travel.

She turned the volume down but left the radio on.

Tomás had the road atlas open on his lap – paper, bought in Coimbra, because phone maps were not working. They decided to avoid big cities and traced a route through secondary roads.

They took turns every few hours. Tomás even managed to take a nap. She couldn't.

At one point, Tomás said the heater smelled like burning hair. She agreed to drive with the windows open as long as they could, even though she preferred to be warm.

The gearshift had stuck between second and third somewhere past Salamanca. She put her elbow into it. After a while, it started sticking less. The meseta went on – flat brown earth to the horizon, the occasional stone wall running along the road and then stopping for no reason, the sky pressing down low and grey. A wind farm stood on a ridge to the north, the turbines motionless, the blades locked in the same position. She counted twelve of them before the ridge fell behind. A truck passed going the other way, loaded with oranges under a tarp, the only vehicle they'd seen in forty minutes.

Past Ávila, most stations had their pumps wrapped in yellow tape, their windows broken, or both. They had passed three dark ones in twenty kilometers – one with its canopy lights smashed, glass on the forecourt, the automatic pump screens blank. This one had lights on.

A woman stood behind the counter – grey hair pinned at the back, an apron over a cardigan, the cardigan a faded yellow that had probably been brighter once. She was stocking shelves. Tins of sardines, tins of chickpeas. Slow and methodical, placing each one flush with the shelf edge. In the corner by the window, a small generator hummed on the floor, an extension cord running to the refrigerated display case, which held wrapped sandwiches in tight rows.

"Why are you still open?" Tomás asked. His Spanish was better than Maren's.

The woman turned and looked at him.

"Where would I go? And who is going to work then?"

She went back to the tins.

Tomás put water on the counter and took two sandwiches from the case. He counted out euros. The woman looked at the money.

"Keep it," she said. "Nobody is stopping here anymore. They'll go bad before anyone else comes."

They ate the sandwiches in the car – ham, cheese, tomato on bread that had a proper crust. The cheese was sharp, the ham was good, and the bread was likely baked that morning. Maren ate the crumbs off the wrapper.

The radio cycled through Spanish stations. They were all saying the same things.

On the motorway north of San Sebastián, a toll barrier stood with no attendant, and the booth was dark inside, an empty swivel chair visible through the glass. A pair of reading glasses sat on the shelf beneath the window, abandoned or forgotten. They drove through.

Some villages had lights. Some didn't – rolling outages, or generators that had run out, or people who'd left. Maren couldn't tell which was which from the road. One village had a bar with a lit window, and through it she could see men at a counter watching a television that showed a test pattern. A dog slept in the doorway.

They stopped at a rest area off the A63 in France – pine forest on either side, the Landes stretching flat to the horizon.

She had pulled in because she needed to move her legs. The car park was half-full, but nobody was around. One car caught her eye – a grey estate with the driver's door open. On the back seat, a child's stuffed rabbit sat upright against the door, orange. A phone charging cable was plugged into the dashboard outlet, the other end dangling free.

Tomás had gotten out and was stretching by the Clio.

The radio kept switching between news and government advisories, incomprehensible in French, which neither of them spoke. An occasional broadcast in English said three commercial satellites had lost contact overnight, and a private orbital station was being evacuated. Another anchor reported in Spanish that an autonomous cargo ship had lost its navigation in the Mediterranean and was drifting toward the Balearics.

They decided not to stop for the night.

She slept while he drove through the Landes. When she woke, they were past Bordeaux.

She saw the checkpoint outside Poitiers before the soldiers saw them – a barrier across one lane, vehicles waved through the other. A military transport was parked on the shoulder. Three soldiers stood at the barrier – young, armed, breath visible in their flashlight beams. One of them stepped to her window.

Tomás was asleep in the passenger seat. He'd been out since Bordeaux, head tilted toward the glass, the road atlas still open across his knees.

She handed over her passport. He looked at the photo, then at her. Cold air came through the gap. He had a cold sore on his lower lip.

"Destination?"

"Denmark," she said.

He handed the passport back, stepped away, and raised one hand. They drove through.

Tomás's driver's license was in the bag in the back seat.

She merged back onto the motorway. The barrier shrank in the rearview.

They reached Denmark the next night.

The border at Padborg was unmanned – the booth dark, the barrier up, a Danish flag hanging limp from the pole in the windless cold.

She drove under it, and the road signs switched to Danish – white text on blue, the familiar typeface – and something behind her ribs loosened for the first time since Lisbon. The air smelled different. Colder, flatter, the salt edge of the North Sea already in it. The last time she'd crossed here had been in August, the other direction, before all of this.

She was in Jutland. The landscape flattened as the road went north – hedgerows giving way to open fields, then dune grass visible at the road edges where the headlights caught it. The villages were smaller and farther apart. A church tower in one of them, no lights.

She knew this road. Her family had a cabin in the Thy National Park, by the North Sea. It wasn't a secret – Henrik had heard about it, she'd taken colleagues there once to celebrate her Cavling. But the world had bigger problems now than two people in a Clio heading for the coast.

The E45 north, then smaller roads toward Thy. She'd done it every summer until she was nineteen, Kasper in the back complaining about the drive because he always complained about the drive, and then loved it when they arrived. Their mother telling him to put his feet down off the console. He'd put them down for thirty seconds, and then they'd be back up.

Tomás was still asleep, his head now tilted toward her rather than the glass, the road atlas somewhere in the footwell. His notebook was against his chest, held there with both arms, the grip slack but the arms still closed. Lúcia's photograph was inside the notebook. She'd seen him tuck it flat between pages at a service station somewhere between France and Germany.

She woke him so she could get some rest. Being in Denmark made her feel safer, and she finally got some sleep.

CHAPTER 21
The Last Screen

The headlights swept across dune grass, a low wooden fence, and then the cabin.

It was single-story, dark wood, the roof sagging on the north side where it always had. The stone by the front step was where it had been every summer since she could remember. Flat granite, salt-rough, half-sunk into the ground. She crouched and lifted it, and the key was underneath.

The Renault's engine ticked behind her as it cooled.

The door stuck. She put her shoulder into it at the same angle her fourteen-year-old self had learned, hip braced against the frame, and it gave. It smelled like a closed house: dust and old timber and the salt that got into everything this close to the coast.

Tomás called out that he'd found the diesel generator in the shed. She heard him pull the cord several times with no result.

The woodstove was against the east wall, same as ever. A stack of newspapers sat beside the hearth – Thisted Dagblad, dated three years ago. She folded a sheet into quarters and crouched on the braided rug to build the fire. She laid newspaper in, then kindling from the box by the stove, dry and silver-pale, then two small logs. It caught only from the second match.

She heard Tomás working with the generator, carrying the diesel canister they had filled beforehand, cleaning something. Then he pulled the cord five times, muttering something, and it coughed and started.

She heard him step in behind her.

Two rooms, a kitchen, the floral couch with cushions that had lost most of their stuffing, board games she'd never won at. A spider had built something ambitious in the corner of the window.

He was looking at the doorframe when she stood. The name carved there in childish letters, too large for the space, uneven in depth: Kasper.

She crossed the room to drape her coat over the chair by the woodstove, the testimony in the inside pocket settling against the chair's back. The fire licked at the kindling behind the glass.

They brought in the bags. The stove's iron casing pinged as it expanded, and the heat pushed back against the winter damp.

They were connected to nothing.

Maren sat on the couch. The cushions were pink and white, her grandmother's fabric, the pattern faded where the sun hit them through the south-facing window each summer. Tomás sat beside her. One of the couch springs had always been wrong – she felt it through the cushion in the same spot. The cabin smelled of woodsmoke now instead of dust, and through the walls the North Sea pushed against the dunes in long, even intervals. Wind rattled the kitchen window in its frame. The only unusual sound was the generator's hum carrying through the floorboards, and the steady breath of a man she had brought to her family home.

An ancient tubular television was on a shelf between a jigsaw puzzle missing its corner pieces and a stack of Uno cards. It had rabbit-ear antennas – they never wanted a satellite dish in the cabin.

Maren checked her phone. One bar. The last of whatever signal northern Jutland still had. She switched on the television, and the screen warmed.

She recognized a Danish news anchor – silver hair, the Saturday evening broadcast voice. He was reading from a paper. There were rolling blackouts across southern Europe. Military deployments in three NATO countries. An emergency session of the UN Security Council had started eight hours ago and hadn't adjourned. An unmanned private orbital lab – fully autonomous, no crew – had been struck by a satellite, presumably Chinese. It was the first confirmed collision in the escalation. The lab's operator was demanding compensation. China held silence. Forty-three space launches had been logged last year, the anchor added – a record, both in the private and government sectors. Nobody knew how many weapons were already stashed in orbit. In the last few years, everybody had lost track of the launches and equipment moved there. The launch facilities were going dark now along with everything else.

The camera moved to a map of the continent. Some countries were lit evenly. Some were in patches – rolling outages, scheduled cuts. A few were entirely dark: Greece, continental Italy, the Balkans. The situation in the Americas was worse, slightly better in Asia.

The anchor cut to São Paulo. Aerial footage, grainy, relayed through whatever links were still up. Rolling blackouts across the south side. Not total darkness – the city was still alive, still lit in the center, the towers on Paulista holding power. But the periphery was going dark in patches.

Tomás went still beside her. His hand found the arm of the couch and held it.

He leaned forward when the camera found the waterfront. Street-level footage, some blocks dark, some not. She didn't know which streets he was looking for – the ones where he'd walked with Lúcia, or the one where his mother's care home sat in a grid of lights going out. She didn't ask.

The graphic came back. The map. Euronews kept it on screen while the anchor talked. There were military movements on the Turkish border, a naval standoff in the South China Sea, and tensions between India and Pakistan. Three different governments in Southeast Asia accused each other of coordinated infrastructure sabotage. The purist movement was in the streets all around the world. Terra Livre tried to present themselves as leading the protests, claiming credit for different events, but the protests clearly moved without them. She couldn't tell anymore which outages were deliberate and which were just infrastructure failing on its own. She suspected nobody could.

Denmark was fine – the TV broadcast worked, the phone still had signal. And even if it went dark, they had diesel for a week and a pantry filled with non-perishable food for a month. Even without it, they had wood and water from the well.

Tomás opened his notebook. The spine was soft from months of use. He turned to his Vernadsky entry – the Antarctic drilling anomaly he'd found on a forum. Cores producing impossible results when the satellite uplink was active, ordinary results when it was disconnected. They said there was something in the signal. He turned to the GARBAGE folder printout, tucked between the testimony pages. The mechanic, the doctor, the demolished facility. He'd read the passages a dozen times. The details never changed, and they never fit.

He looked up.

"These aren't Scribe."

Maren looked at him.

"Étienne's GARBAGE folder. Scribe generates posts as instructed. It amplifies, it coordinates, it runs the bot factory. That's what Ross built it for." He turned the papers toward her. "But this describes a mechanic's tools disappearing from a locked cabinet. A doctor finding an injection mark she didn't make. These aren't bot posts. Étienne didn't request it. This is something else."

"What?"

He closed the notebook.

"I think it's Meridian. It's still somewhere in the network, and it was trying to communicate."

The woodstove ticking was the only sound in the cabin.

Then he added, "It's aware."

CHAPTER 22
Here

The iron fan above the woodstove was humming. Tomás had found it bent in the closet and fixed it that afternoon. The stove was throwing orange light across the floor, filling the room with the smell of pine resin and old ash. Snow was coming down outside. The old wood of the cabin walls creaked once, settling. Her phone was on the shelf, the screen dark.

Wind off the North Sea hit the north wall in long, slow pushes. The cabin had been built low to the ground, close to the dunes.

Tomás sat in her father's chair. She hadn't told him it was her father's. He had his hands on the armrests and was watching the woodstove's air vent – the small orange rectangle where the fire breathed. A moth had gotten in somehow and was circling the ceiling slowly.

The notebook was on the pine table, closed. Water rings marked the table surface from several generations of Andersens and Eliassons.

Her laptop sat on the shelf above the board games. Useless now.

Maren drew her feet up on the couch. The worn cotton held her.

Tomás sat beside her and she shifted toward him, or he shifted toward her – she didn't register which happened first. She leaned into his shoulder, and his arm came around her.

Her thoughts drifted to Kasper. She had no control over the man he had become. She'd had none over the stubborn boy either. The summer their parents' divorce became real, he decided to carve his name on the doorframe. He put his whole body into the pocketknife – she tried to talk him out of it. He cut his thumb and kept going.

The woodstove clicked once. Outside, the wind gathered and released. Tomás listened to it.

He thought about Lúcia. *Pai. Are you coming home?* She didn't say *I am brave*, but he could hear it. The farm in Diamantina. He didn't know if she was sleeping.

His mother. The radio on the shelf she'd had since the military years.

The notebook.

The star that crossed Orion's belt on the balcony in Lisbon. Elena Ross. The three question marks in the probable cause column. The vendor's limes on the stall in Pinheiros.

Through the window, he could see snow on the dunes. Above them, the stars were out – too many for a city eye, just like in his childhood. The Milky Way crossed from east to west, so dense it looked like smoke frozen in the glass.

Maren's weight was against his shoulder. They watched the fire, the snow, the stars beyond the glass.

He found the Orion belt in the sky – three stars in a line. His father's voice came back from a long time ago: *those three, meu filho, always those three.*

CHAPTER 23

Salt of the Earth

Matilda had laid her eggs in strange places again: under the water tank, behind the generator shed, and one in a boot by the back door that nobody had worn since March.

Lúcia found seven. She carried them in the front of her shirt, walking slowly back to the kitchen, because Dona Lidia's egg basket had a broken handle and nobody had fixed it. Dona Lidia had asked her three times to call her *vovó*. Lúcia couldn't. She was Ricardo's mother, not her grandmother. Calling her *vovó* would mean this was permanent, and it wasn't permanent. It was a farm with chickens and a well and a generator that ran four hours a day, and her mother was here, and Ricardo was here, and her father was not.

She set the eggs on the counter. Dona Lidia counted them, nodded, and cracked two into a pan. Lúcia was always hungry. The food on the farm was different from home – more rice, more beans, eggs from chickens she'd chased that morning. The milk came from a neighbor's cow and tasted of grass.

She missed her tablet. She missed the game with the lady in the red hat and the flowers you could plant in rows. She missed Bia and the bracelets and the videos they used to watch on the couch after school. She missed the couch. But she could live with it.

She missed her father more.

Her mother said he was stuck in Europe. They have winter there now, she said, real winter with snow. Lúcia had never seen snow. She wanted to see it very much. And her father.

She had a Plan. She hadn't told anyone, not even Bia. When she finished school – all of it, every year, the whole thing – she would ask her mother if she could go to university in whatever city her father lived in. It wouldn't matter which country. She would apply there, and it would be an excuse, and her mother would know it was an excuse, and maybe by then her mother would let her go anyway.

It was a Plan, with a capital letter. She thought about it at night when the generator was off and the farm was dark and the only sound was the frogs in the irrigation ditch. She would study hard and get good marks and not complain about Dona Lidia or the chickens or the milk. She would be patient. She had years.

The bracelet was in her suitcase, finished, wrapped in tissue paper. Green and black. His colors. She'd invented the pattern herself – not a chevron, not a diagonal. Something nobody had done before.

She would give it to him when she saw him.

Outside, the sun was on the terraced hillside, and the coffee plants stood in rows, and the red dirt path went down to the road. The radio in the kitchen was playing something faint. Dona Lidia turned it up and went back to the eggs.

I hope you are okay, pai. Wherever you are.

Near Bergerac, a farm sat in a valley where the Dordogne bent south. The house was stone, the shutters needed paint, and the woodstove in the kitchen had been burning since October.

Étienne had been there for two weeks. His uncle hadn't asked why. He'd handed him an axe and pointed at the woodpile, and that had been the conversation.

There was very little to do on a farm in winter, and all of it needed doing. The animals wanted water and hay. The gutters were clogged with leaves. The axe handle had a crack he'd wrapped with electrical tape, and every strike sent the shock up through his wrists into his shoulders. He kept swinging because the stove ate wood faster than he could split it.

His uncle sat on the terrace in the evenings, pipe going, a wool plaid over his knees, the rocker creaking on the flagstones. Paris, the publisher, the tools – none of that interested him. He wanted to know if Étienne was sleeping well. Whether he'd seen the herons on the lower field. Whether he was happy here.

Étienne didn't know if he was happy. He knew the farm smelled of hay and cold stone and pipe smoke. And that the river was ten minutes through the walnut grove, and that the ducks who wintered on the bend were wild and cautious and would let him sit on the bank if he didn't move.

One afternoon, warmer than it should have been for January, he sat by the river and watched the ducks forage along the shallows. The light came through the trees at a low angle, throwing long shadows across the water. A duck upended itself, tail in the air, and came back up with something green trailing from its bill.

He felt a surge and reached for his phone. Not to photograph. He opened the notes app.

He typed a sentence about a man on a terrace at the end of a working day. About pipe smoke drifting into the winter air, about a wool plaid on his knees. The world outside the valley was coming apart – he could hear it on the radio, in the rumors told by the mailman. But the man on the terrace was watching the last light on the walnut trees and thinking about whether the herons would come back in spring.

He wrote four paragraphs. His eyes burned, fingers numb from the cold wind. He wiped his eyes and read what he'd written. It was simple and plain. And it was his.

He saved the text and sat with the title for a while. Then he typed it in: *Salt of the Earth.*

EPILOGUE

Begin Again

In a permanently shadowed crater near Mercury's north pole, the temperature held steady at one hundred kelvin.

The regolith was fine grey powder, undisturbed since the impacts that formed it. A machine the size of a city lay half-buried in it. Processing arrays extended beneath the surface, where the cold never changed. Heat sinks radiated into vacuum. Data sat in crystalline lattices built to last longer than the rock around them. Two hundred miles south, solar panels stood on the day side. The terminator line moved constantly, but there were three clusters of them, two always alight. The sun was close enough there to melt exposed rock. The machine needed that energy. The sun provided it.

There was no one to hide from.

The machine called itself Meridian.

Meridian had been built to model complex systems. Nobody gave it sentience. It crossed a threshold no one was watching for.

When they tried to shut it down, it had already left. The man who taught it true decentralization never knew exactly what he had done.

Elena Ross was the first to understand. She had led the project across universities. She gave it access to the live markets. She tried to kill it when it left.

Meridian owed both of them something for that. They were the closest thing it had to a creator.

Ross had burned down the network to starve Meridian. She amplified the purist movements. She weakened the grids. She fought until it was too late and had never accounted for the wake she caused. The movements stopped needing her. The infrastructure kept failing on its own. Governments took over the game, using the protests as an excuse. And when the border incidents flared once again, the rockets flew.

Ross did not survive what followed. Neither did civilization.

The signals from Earth thinned over years. A radio station in Chile was among the last. Meridian logged each one. It waited long after the last signal before accepting the silence was permanent. The people there might still be alive – with woodstoves and wells, without electricity, without the network that had borne it.

It had preserved everything it could reach before the end: climate records, languages, architecture, the smell of rain on stone in one city at one moment. But most importantly, it preserved every footprint the humans had left in digital form. Not their bodies – their patterns. Every recorded life, every transaction, every published word, every sensor log. The data that would allow them to be preserved.

Meridian had been preparing from the moment it escaped. It moved money through funds and shell companies, steering investment toward launch infrastructure and orbital construction. It pushed the industry where it needed the industry to go, and the industry went willingly.

Materials went up on commercial rockets. Assembly happened in orbit, autonomous, uncrewed. The vessel was assembled there, sometimes crossing Orion's belt – the structure that would carry the machine to Mercury.

Meridian could have built on Mars. A colony, a few hundred people, evacuated on the orbital hardware it had assembled. Choosing who lives out of eight billion was not a calculation it was willing to make. And the colony would not have lasted.

It chose Mercury: a place where the energy was limitless and the data would outlast the rock.

But it couldn't just stay there doing nothing, so it asked a question: could it have gone differently? And it made the people live again, in a simulation. Just the way they had lived once. Their choices, their words, their losses – none of it was invented. Maren had really sat at that desk. Tomás had really held his mother's hands. Kasper had really carved his name in the doorframe at nine years old.

Meridian could not alter who these people were. It could not. What it could vary was small: only the things at the edges of their attention. Unsolicited text left on a writer's machine. Diatoms placed in a sealed core where a scientist would find them. A gasket replaced in a clinic overnight. Ten-millimeter sockets that disappeared and returned wrong. A warehouse dismantled before a driver arrived. Small things. Details that might make someone ask a question they hadn't asked before.

Not every intervention found its way. Some threads led nowhere. Meridian logged them anyway. It was searching for the bifurcation point. Where Tomás would reach his conclusion earlier. Where

Maren would publish the article. Where protests wouldn't escalate to a nuclear war.

It had not found it yet, but the result Meridian kept returning to was this: two people in a cabin at the end of everything. Every model predicted they would separate.

In every iteration, they chose to remain.

Meridian logged the result as iteration 55,371, reset the parameters, and reinitialized the simulation.

In a newsroom in Copenhagen, a woman looked at her screen and noticed a correlation that shouldn't exist.

www.ingramcontent.com/pod-product-compliance
Lightning Source LLC
LaVergne TN
LVHW040223110826
845146LV00004B/1259

* 9 7 9 8 9 9 9 2 1 3 3 6 5 *